Highe

San Diego After Dark

Tess Summers

Copyright 2025 by Tess Summers

Published: 2025

Published by Seasons Press LLC.

ISBN: 9798289714725

Copyright © 2025, Tess Summers.

Edited by Maggie Ryan.

Cover by OliviaProDesign.

All rights reserved. No part of this publication may be reproduced, stored in a retrieval system, or transmitted in any form or by any means, electronic, mechanical, recording, or otherwise, without the prior written permission of the author, except in the case of brief quotations within critical reviews and otherwise as permitted by copyright law.

NO AI TRAINING: Without in any way limiting the author's exclusive rights under copyright, any use of this publication to "train" generative artificial intelligence (AI) technologies to generate text is expressly prohibited. The author reserves all rights to license uses of this work for generative AI training and development of machine learning language models.

This is a work of fiction. The characters, incidents and dialogues in this book are of the author's imagination and are not to be construed as real. Any resemblance to actual events or persons, living or dead, is completely coincidental.

This book is for mature readers. It contains sexually explicit scenes and graphic language that may be considered offensive by some.

All sexually active characters in this work are eighteen years of age or older.

Blurb

I didn't lose the girl—I bought her.

She turned me down at a masquerade party, then gave herself to someone else.

So when she put herself up for auction, I made sure I was the highest bidder.

I didn't do it to protect her, I wanted to own her.

To punish her; remind her who she rejected.

I told myself it was a transaction. Nothing more.

But Vivian didn't respond the way she was supposed to.

She obeyed. She submitted. She smiled like she wasn't afraid of me—and I hated how much I liked that.

She was never supposed to matter.

Then she walked away.

Now I can't stop thinking about her. The girl I tried to break is the one who broke me.

And I'll do whatever it takes to get her back.

Table of Contents

Blurb iii
Important Note to Potential Readers 1
Prologue 2
Chapter One 6
Chapter Two 13
Chapter Three 22
Chapter Four 29
Chapter Five 31
Chapter Six 36
Chapter Seven 38
Chapter Eight 44
Chapter Nine 51
Chapter Ten 60
Chapter Eleven 64
Chapter Twelve 70
Chapter Thirteen 75
Chapter Fourteen 83
Chapter Fifteen 89
Chapter Sixteen 98
Chapter Seventeen 103
Chapter Eighteen 111
Chapter Nineteen 115
Chapter Twenty 124
Chapter Twenty-One 127
Chapter Twenty-Two 135

Chapter Twenty-Three	140
Chapter Twenty-Four	147
Chapter Twenty-Five	154
Chapter Twenty-Six	159
Chapter Twenty-Seven	163
Epilogue	167
Thank you	170
Acknowledgments	171
Breakfast Is Served	172
San Diego Social Scene	173
Agents of Ensenada	174
Boston's Elite series	175
Wounded Heroes	176
The Mister Series	176
About the Author	177
Contact Me!	177

Important Note to Potential Readers

Harvard studies have shown trigger warnings may cause more harm than good, so the only warning I'll provide is this: if you're a reader who needs trigger warnings, **do not read this book.**

I cannot stress this enough.

There is so much morally corrupt and/or legally questionable shit in this story, it's not funny. It is not your typical Tess Summers book.

You've been warned.

On a sidenote, it does have an HEA, so there's that.

Highest Bidder
San Diego After Dark

Prologue

Vivian

"I'm sorry, you caught him doing what?" my best friend, Kit, screeched through the phone.

"Stealing money from my purse."

"Again?"

"Yeah," I said with a sigh. "But hey, at least he wasn't going to buy drugs with it this time. It was for scratchers at the corner store. Allegedly."

"Please tell me you are done with this guy for good, Viv."

"I'm done with him for good. I'd been over him for a while, to be honest. I just needed a reason to end it."

"You mean pawning your tablet and stealing money from your purse the first time wasn't enough of a reason?"

"I don't know—I mean, yes, you're right. But he'd groveled and tried to make amends by buying the tablet back. I thought it'd be bitchy if I said I forgave him if I really hadn't."

"Who the fuck cares if it's bitchy? He needed a bitch *slap*! Why do you keep dating losers?"

"My therapist says it's because they're familiar. Textbook daddy issues. But in my defense, I didn't realize Trent was a loser until recently."

I could practically see my BFF's eyeroll over the phone when she snarked, "The lizard tattoo on his neck wasn't enough of a giveaway?"

"I thought he was edgy."

"He was something, all right. But perfect timing, breaking up with him! My club's having their monthly masquerade party this Friday. I can bring a guest if you want to go."

Kit bartended at an upscale sex club. I wasn't sure if that was an oxymoron or not, but it cost a hundred grand a year in annual dues, plus a monthly minimum that members had to spend at the club. Which was why Kit made a killing slinging drinks there—people trying to run up their bar tab to satisfy the requirement.

"Are you working that night or playing?"

"Playing. We're supposed to wear masks, so hopefully none of the regulars will recognize me. Plus, the anonymity makes it hotter."

"I don't know. Some of the stories you've told me... I think I'd feel like Alice when she fell down the rabbit hole."

"It's no different than having a one-night stand. Except the chances that the guy you're hooking up with will be a kinky multi-millionaire are almost one hundred percent. And the club vets its members, so you know you'll be safe."

"Does that mean they're going to vet me, too?"

"Don't worry—it's pretty straightforward. They'll want your ID, and I'll have to vouch for you. And you'll have to get tested when you come in to sign some paperwork agreeing to the club's rules. After that, you're good to go."

"That sounds like a lot of work to attend an orgy."

She sighed because she'd already told me a dozen times. "It's not an orgy. There've only been a few instances where it bordered on being able to call it that. Most of the time, people just hook up with one or two people."

"Can I think about it?"

"Yeah, but don't think too long. If you don't want to go, I'm not going to waste my plus-one."

"Okay, I'll let you know in the morning."

"It really is fun. And there's zero pressure to do anything you're not comfortable with. They have different colored wristbands to show what you're into."

"Different colors? Like, for what?"

"Well, yellow means you're down for a golden shower. Red means you're into spanking. Red with black dots means you want to be flogged or whipped. Black means you're up for anything. Pink means you're curious and open to discussion. White means you're just there to watch. There are other colors, but I can't remember what they mean right now. There's a whole sheet explaining it when you check in."

"What color do you wear?"

"Depends on my mood. I did the golden shower thing once, just to say I tried it. It wasn't my favorite, but I could see why some people have the kink. There's a definite power dynamic to it."

"Hmm. I like being dominated, but I don't want to get peed on. Maybe some light spanking. Definitely not flogged."

"I think you should wear a pink bracelet. You know, if you decide to come."

We both knew I was going to say yes, but I needed to keep up the ruse.

"I'll let you know tomorrow."

Chapter One

Vivian

I fidgeted with the pink silk ribbon around my left wrist as Kit and I made our way further inside the club. I'd decided to wear it on my left, to avoid drawing attention to the phoenix tattoo on the inside of my right wrist.

I was glad my friend knew exactly where to go and what to do because I felt like a fish out of water.

Even when Kit told me she worked at an "upscale" sex club, I'd envisioned something like the strip club I worked in: neon lights, sticky floors, a couple of disco balls, red vinyl booths with slits down the center that exposed the foam underneath. That was not the case at Velvet Underground.

I'd never seen anything like it. Even the air smelled expensive, like spiced rum and cedarwood.

Everything dripped luxury, from the soft lighting to the dark wood and gold trim. The purple velvet seating seemed so plush, I was afraid if I sat in a booth, I'd sink in and disappear. Gold velvet curtains framed private booths, and the bar looked like it belonged in a five-star hotel.

I think everyone wearing fancy masks while elegantly dressed in black tie and evening gowns added to the glamor of the night. I half-expected to see Jay Gatsby and Nick Carraway drinking martinis at the bar.

"Wow. So, this is where you work."

Kit grinned under her pink feathered and jeweled mask that matched her dress and lipstick perfectly.

"It's pretty over the top, I know."

I made a point of surveying our surroundings. "It's beautiful, though."

She glanced around, too.

"Yeah, seeing it through your eyes makes me appreciate it again. I think being here four nights a week has made me blind to the sheer opulence of the place."

I looked down at the sequined white dress I'd found at Goodwill to match the white Venetian mask with rhinestones that Kit had bought for me. It covered the upper half of my face, but even hiding behind a mask, one thing was clear—I didn't belong here.

We'd barely stepped up to the bar when a tall, dark-haired man wearing the hell out of a tux appeared at my side. He had on a black domino mask, which seemed to be the mask of choice tonight for the men. A few were sporting *Phantom of the Opera*-style half-masks, and a couple had ornately decorated Venetian masks, but they were in the minority by far.

It was almost as if the club had handed out domino masks at the door to any guy who'd arrived without one and wouldn't let them in unless they put it on. (A theory Kit later confirmed.)

"Well, hello. Aren't you a breath of fresh air."

I smiled at the handsome stranger. "And aren't you the charmer."

"Can I buy you a drink, maybe get to know you a little better?"

Before I had a chance to accept his offer, Kit interjected. "We just got here, so we're going to mingle for a while before we 'get to know' anyone."

He chuckled, undeterred.

"Fair enough. But still, let me buy you both a drink."

I was pretty sure with Kit working here, her fellow bartenders would hook us up with free booze, but she smiled and said, "That's very kind, thank you," then ordered us two glasses of champagne as he told the bartender, "Put those on my tab."

While we waited for our drinks, the stranger asked, "So, will I have the pleasure of bidding on a date with either of you ladies next week?"

Again, Kit answered for me. "No, we're just here for the party tonight."

He raked his gaze up and down my body, then rested it on my tits when he replied, "What a pity. Then I definitely hope we can chat later."

"I look forward to it."

He walked away, and Kit leaned over and told me, "You will not be "chatting" with Grayson DeLuca later. That man would eat you up and spit you out!"

"Isn't that the point of why we're here?"

"Trust me on this."

"Of course I trust you. You know these men, I don't. We should have a signal for who you approve of and who you don't. Like you scratch your chin if they're a nay, and tug on your ear if they're a yay."

She laughed. "Or, how about I just subtly shake my head yes or no?"

I grinned. "That works, too."

The bartender appeared with our glasses of bubbly and winked at Kit before he put them down, like he was letting her know he knew who she was.

We lifted the flutes in a toast.

"To new adventures," I said with a confident smile, although it felt like a kaleidoscope of butterflies had taken flight in my stomach as I thought about what those adventures tonight might entail.

"To new adventures," Kit echoed then clinked her glass against mine.

"So, what's this auction Grayson was talking about?" I asked before taking a sip of champagne.

My friend had been in the middle of a drink and choked when my question came out, making her pat her chest. After she recovered, she murmured, "Baby steps, sweetie. We're starting you on the bunny slopes tonight. An auction is the equivalent of a black-diamond run."

****

Jeff

I'd almost skipped tonight's party, but the moment I saw her from across the room, I congratulated myself for deciding to come after all. She looked like an angel in her white dress with sequins glinting under the lights. Half her face was hidden by a mask, and I couldn't help but want to get closer.

Then I saw DeLuca approach her at the bar, at least, I was pretty sure it was Grayson, and decided to hang back and observe from the other end. Hopefully I hadn't missed my shot by moving too slowly.

I watched her companion smile and shake her head, then a minute later, DeLuca nodded and walked off.

That's right. Move along.

She's *my* angel.

Hopefully.

At least for tonight.

The vision in white was laughing with her friend, champagne glass in hand, head tilted back as if she didn't have a care in the world.

She caught me watching her, and I raised my glass in a silent toast. She lifted hers in return, a shy smile playing at the corners of her mouth. That was all the invitation I needed to make my way over. I stepped away from the bar and weaved through the crowd, never taking my eyes off her.

Her blonde hair caught the light like a halo as she laughed at something her friend said. She tucked it behind her ear while her lips tugged into a smile that looked practiced. Every move she made felt deliberate, like she knew eyes were on her and she was performing. Maybe for me, and I didn't mind one bit.

Her eyes found mine again, and I didn't hesitate to step in closer.

She turned to face me, and her smile faltered, barely, but I caught it. She didn't seem afraid. Hesitant, maybe, but not scared. Maybe she was deciding how much trouble I was.

Smart girl.

But she pulled her shoulders back and lifted her chin when she looked me in the eye, and I knew she had some sass.

Just my type. Those were more fun to break.

I let my gaze drop to the pink ribbon on her left wrist and lightly brushed my thumb over it. "Pink ribbon," I murmured, eyes locked on hers. "Curious and open. I like that."

Then I noticed the hand holding her champagne flute, more specifically, the phoenix inked on her right wrist. "But *this* has *me* curious," I murmured, taking her glass and setting it on the bar so I could lift her hand and press a soft kiss to the tattoo. "I'd love to know the story behind it."

She didn't pull away, which I took as a good sign, even as she replied, "That's a conversation for another time."

"Good. It means there'll be another time."

She gave me a wicked smile. "But I thought tonight was more of a one-night-only kind of party."

I leaned in closer. "Then I guess I'll have to make tonight count."

She let out a soft laugh, her eyes dancing. "Oh, I have a feeling you will."

I lowered my head, the smell of her citrusy shampoo mixed with her floral perfume tantalized my senses as I let my lips brush her ear. "Then let's find somewhere a little more... private. Somewhere we can get to know each other better without all the noise."

She glanced at her friend, who I noticed gave her a subtle headshake, before she turned back to me with an apologetic smile. "I don't think so."

Well, that wasn't what I was expecting.

I stepped back and held her gaze for a beat. I could almost feel the disappointment rolling off her. Or maybe that was my own.

"What a shame." I nodded my head at her, then toward her friend—who I was pretty sure was Kit, the bartender. I don't know what her problem with me was, I always tipped well. "Enjoy your evening, ladies." I turned and walked away to scope out the rest of the prospects.

But I couldn't help but look back. She was still watching me. Still calm. Still sassy.

I liked that probably more than I should've.

I took another lap around the room, drink in hand, pretending I was scouting options. But the truth?

None of them intrigued me the way she had.

That didn't mean I was going home unfulfilled. I'd come here to scratch an itch, not catch feelings.

So, when a leggy brunette with a grey bracelet straddled my lap without asking, I let her. My dick might've been disappointed earlier, but he wasn't picky.

Chapter Two

Vivian

The minute I locked eyes with the masked, sandy blond stranger from across the bar, I felt both intrigued and intimidated.

After I raised my champagne flute in response to his silent toast, he started toward me.

His tuxedo hugged his broad shoulders and lean body, the black fabric catching the low lights of the club. He moved with the grace of a panther stalking its prey, and I had to will myself not to run.

Up close, his blue eyes beneath the black domino mask were sharp and knowing, as if he could see straight through me and tell I didn't belong.

But as we talked, I caught a twinkle of mischief in his baby blues. That hint of playfulness put me at ease, like maybe he didn't mind that I didn't quite fit in.

I felt such an attraction to him that I almost took his hand anyway after Kit shook her head.

As I watched him walk away, I had an urge to run after him until my friend's voice stopped me. "Honey, I know you're disappointed, but Dr. Connolly's reputation is even worse than DeLuca's."

"How so?"

"He has a cruel streak."

"Oh." I glanced in the direction he had just disappeared. "Really? I didn't get that vibe from him."

"I mean, I don't have firsthand knowledge, but I've heard some of the more 'seasoned' female members caution newer women about him. But his good looks and charm make them throw caution to the wind, and they usually end up crying over him in the bathroom."

That didn't necessarily mean he was cruel.

"So, he comes here a lot."

"Well, yeah. You don't spend the kind of money it costs to be a member here and not come." She grinned at me. "In both senses of the word."

I don't know why the idea of him being here a lot bothered me as much as it did. I had no room to judge. Two nights and two afternoons a week, I paraded around in nothing but a G-string, pasties, and four-inch heels for a living, grinding on men's laps until they came in their pants.

Kit signaled to the bartender for another round, and when we got our fresh glasses, she suggested, "Wanna go walk around?"

****

Jeff

The chick currently in my lap wore a grey bracelet to signify free use and/or consensual nonconsent. Some forceful sex might help me take my mind off the little Phoenix who'd turned me down.

Grey Bracelet's mouth tasted sweet, like the champagne we'd been drinking, along with a hint of vanilla from her red lipstick that I was sure was all over my face.

Hopefully, it'd be all over my dick, too, before it was completely smeared off her mouth.

I'd had a kink about that ever since my first lipstick party with the pledges of my fraternity's sister sorority. The more dicks they sucked, the better their chances of getting in.

Completely unethical, yeah, and I hadn't given a shit.

I still didn't.

Ethics were for poor people who couldn't buy their way out of trouble.

Let me stop you right there before you decide what an asshole I am. Okay, no, I am an asshole—you're right about that, at least when it comes to women. But I do have *some* ethics. Like when it comes to my job, I'm aboveboard, one hundred percent of the time. Hell, I even have compassion for my patients. And I do care about other people, for the most part. I know how to be a functioning member of a civilized society.

I even fucking recycle, for chrissake.

But, ever since college when I'd discovered that most women, or at least the sorority sluts I hung around with, were more interested in money than what kind of person you are, my morality meter broke. If it was technically legal and I thought I could get away with it, I did it.

Fucking my date's sorority sister in the ass in a dark corner of the frat house while my date stood in line to go to the bathroom at a party? Yep, I did that. Fingering my frat brother's girlfriend then coming down her throat as he watched a football game in the next room while she "gave me a haircut"? Check. Making amends to said frat brother after his girlfriend confessed our tryst by blackmailing Judith Walker, our smoking hot BioChem professor with photos of me balls deep inside her so she'd give him a passing grade in her class? Check check.

I'm a bastard.

One thing though that I would never do is tell a girl I love her or lead her to believe there was a future with me. Every chick I'd been with knew she was nothing special, although I suspected they all believed they'd be the one to change me.

Sure, I'd thought about settling down. Maybe having a kid or two. I'd even tried dating "nice girls". Ones I could see taking home to meet the parents. But my deviant desires usually brought things to an end pretty quickly, sending me back to the women who could fulfill my dark desires but not have a future with.

Thank god I found Velvet Underground not long after landing my job at the VA in San Diego. I knew frequenting prostitutes—even high-end ones, was going to land me in jail one day. Then I'd lose my job, and I loved my job.

Out of the corner of my eye, I caught a flash of white. Breaking the kiss, I noticed Phoenix talking to Tyler Stevens. His dad had been one of the OGs in Silicon Valley and left his billions to his four kids. The three oldest were from his first wife and had been groomed to take over the company. But Tyler's mom was Stevens' much younger trophy wife, so he grew up differently than his siblings. Pretty much the only thing the little prick was equipped to do was live off his trust fund. His days consisted of golfing or surfing and his nights were spent partying.

I had no problem with trust fund kids, hell, I was one of them. But at least do something with your life, man.

The dude's hand came around Phoenix's back and roved to her ass.

Seriously?

She was going to hook up with *him* instead of me?

While she was technically talking to Tyler, I noticed her attention drifted my way more often than it should.

Good.

Holding Phoenix's gaze, I spun Grey Bracelet around in my lap so she faced the room, then spread her legs and lifted her dress. I traced an index finger down the seam of her pussy and chuckled in her ear, "You naughty slut. You're not wearing any panties. Everyone in the room can see your wet cunt."

Grey Bracelet moaned, but I wasn't looking at her. I was still watching Phoenix for her reaction.

She stilled. Her smile didn't slip, not exactly. But something shifted. A flicker in her eyes.

There it was. That crack.

"You should probably punish me," Grey Bracelet whispered, squirming on my lap.

"Yeah, baby. I probably should," I replied, not breaking eye contact with the one who mattered.

I let my fingers trail up higher, spreading her wider, making sure Phoenix could see exactly what she'd turned down.

And then I smiled.

Right at her.

The kind of smile that said *I hope this fucking hurts.*

Phoenix's lips parted, and her brows dipped briefly. Most people would've missed it.

I didn't.

The little shift in her expression, the stiff set of her shoulders. Like she was trying not to care.

But she cared.

She fucking cared.

That flash of something—disappointment, maybe even jealousy—was all I needed.

I tapped Grey Bracelet's thigh. "Get up," I murmured. "Let's go finish this elsewhere where I can properly punish you."

She got up, eager and oblivious, but I wasn't thinking about her.

I was thinking about the girl in white, trying to pretend she wasn't watching me walk away with another woman.

Pretending it didn't bother her.

But it did.

And we both knew it.

That made me feel lighter as Grey Bracelet's heels clacked down the hall.

Maybe I'd only hurt her a little now.

****

Vivian

Even though I wanted to, I didn't leave after he walked away

Not that he noticed. He was already halfway across the room with Grey Bracelet Girl and her long legs, red lipstick, and no panties.

I shouldn't have cared. Hell, I'd barely met him. I didn't know his first name, or if I even liked him.

But I kept replaying the way he'd looked at me. The way his lips had brushed my wrist and sent shivers down my spine. The way my body had leaned in like it already knew what he could do.

Now he was giving that to someone else, without hesitation.

I couldn't be mad he was hooking up with someone else—that's what this party was all about. Besides, I was the one who'd said no.

But the way he took the rejection like it didn't matter, like I was just one more pretty girl in a mask... that had stung my pride a little.

I decided I came here to get laid, and I wasn't leaving until it happened.

I let the frat bro in the blue half-mask hover for one more drink, but Kit didn't need to give me the *no* signal for that guy. The minute he told me, "This place is full of women trying too hard. I figured I'd give the understated ones a shot tonight," I'd given him a "fuck you" smile and headed back to the bar without so much as a "Later, loser."

That's where the man in the silver mask approached me. He was tall, dark, and confident without projecting arrogance. He didn't leer or posture, just stood there, calm and quiet, waiting for me to speak first. As if he knew better than to move too fast.

Kit noticed him next to me and gave a subtle nod.

I'd been waiting all night for her nod. For a while, I thought it would never come. But finally, there it was.

I felt a mix of relief, and something else. Regret maybe. Like maybe it'd come too late.

But I had it now. That's what mattered.

So, when Silver Mask offered to buy me a drink, I said yes. And yes to another.

Not necessarily because I wanted *him*. But because he looked at me like it was worth the effort to pursue me. And I needed to feel that; I needed to feel wanted.

It wasn't fair to be disappointed that Dr. Connolly walked away when I was the one who'd said no. But part of me still wished he would've tried harder. Like I'd mattered enough to be chased.

Instead, he looked me in the eye while he touched someone else. That wasn't just walking away. That was a middle finger. Message received—loud and clear.

I didn't ask for Silver Mask's name, per the club's rules, and after a few drinks, we ended up in one of the private rooms with the gold velvet curtains drawn.

I got on top and took what I needed, coming just before he did.

He groaned when he came, with his hands gripping my hips. It was controlling and hot, but nothing like I imagined the good doctor would have been.

Nothing like how I thought he would have made me feel.

I slid off Silver Mask before he caught his breath, pulled my dress down, and left without a word.

I walked through my apartment door feeling unsatisfied, like I'd ordered the wrong thing off the menu and tried to convince myself it hit the spot.

It hadn't. But it'd have to do.

At least I got an orgasm, I suppose.

Chapter Three

Vivian

I woke to the sound of someone pounding on my door. *Bam! Bam! Bam!* Followed by my sister's voice urgently calling my name from the hall.

What the heck time is it?

I moaned when I rolled off my couch, still in my pajamas, and padded barefoot across the worn linoleum toward the door. My mouth felt like it had cotton in it and my teeth were in serious need of brushing and maybe some mouthwash.

Another round of pounding matched the thumping in my head. I'd had too much champagne last night and not enough food.

"Jesus, I'm coming. Chill."

I froze when I opened the door and found my little sister's face blotchy with tears and streaked mascara. Her hoodie was unzipped over a tank top that looked like she might have slept in it.

"Hope? What's going on?"

She answered my question with a question. "Can I come in?"

She didn't wait for me to say yes—just brushed past and collapsed onto my couch, tucking her toes under her body and pulling her legs into her hoodie.

"What happened?" I closed the door behind her, my heart thudding. "Is it Mom?"

She shook her head. "No. I mean—not yet."

"What the hell does that mean?"

Her wide eyes brimmed with tears when she looked over at me. "It's Dad. The people he owed money to—they came to the house."

I stared at her. "I don't understand. Dad's dead."

"Yeah, well he ended up leaving us an inheritance after all. His loan shark debt."

I sat down hard, the couch springs creaking beneath me. "You've got to be kidding me."

She wrapped her arms around her legs and rested her chin on her knees. "He owed a lot of money to the wrong people, Viv. They said if we don't pay, they'll come back."

"How do they expect you to pay? The son of a bitch left you with nothing."

"Do you think a guy named Lorenzo with a face full of scars and two goons in matching leather jackets give a shit?"

My stomach dropped. "Did they threaten you?"

"Not directly. But they weren't exactly subtle. Lorenzo said it'd be a real shame if something happened to Mom's car. Or the dog. Or her fingers."

"Jesus Christ."

Hope wiped her nose with her sleeve. "Mom didn't want to tell you because it would just give you one more reason to hate Dad. But I didn't know where else to go. Viv, they started talking about Roscoe and Mom's fingers!"

My throbbing head made it hard to think. Or maybe it was my rage that had my thoughts jumbled all over the place.

That son of a bitch was still fucking over my mom, even from the grave. She was right about one thing: it was one more thing to add to the list of reasons why I despised my father, even in death.

"Did they say how much time they'd give you?"

"They said we needed to make a payment by Monday."

"Did they say how much?"

"He said nothing less than a thousand. And that's just covering the juice."

"What's the total amount?"

"Eighty-seven grand. Give or take."

There was no way we'd ever come up with enough money to get out of that debt. We'd just be making thousand-dollar payments every few weeks in perpetuity.

My eyes dropped to the phoenix tattoo on my wrist, the one I'd gotten the day I'd saved enough money to stop couch surfing and sign the lease on my first apartment. A tiny studio that smelled like old coffee, stale cigarettes, and freedom. I'd sworn that day I'd be out from under my father's thumb forever.

And yet, here he was, pressing down on my neck from the grave.

Funny, I'd gotten the tattoo to mark the day I'd started my new life. Now I just had a growing sense that maybe I'd never really risen from anything. The ashes were still there.

"We'll figure something out. I can come up with the thousand by Monday. At least that'll buy us a little time."

She sniffled. "I'm sorry to dump this on you—"

I cut her off. "You're not the one dumping this on me. It was dumped on you, same as it was on Mom, courtesy of dear old Dad. I wish I could say I was surprised."

We sat in silence. She leaned her head on my shoulder, and for a second, it felt like we were kids again, hiding in the closet during one of Dad's tirades, hoping he'd pass out before he found us.

The sunlight slanting through the blinds told me it was already afternoon. I kissed her temple and sat up.

"You're welcome to hang out here, but I have to head into work for a bit."

If I hurried, I could get to the club and talk to my boss about some extra shifts before things got busy.

~~~~

I hadn't had to worry about Club Allure being too busy for Rico to talk to me. It was technically open, but I'd barely even call it that.

A few regulars were parked at the bar with their attention divided between some college football game on the flatscreens above the shelves of cheap liquor and the bored-looking girl onstage who was half-heartedly twirling on the pole in pasties and heels.

I walked past her and made my way to where Rico was perched on his usual stool in the corner of the bar. He had the weekly schedule in one hand, his gaze bouncing between it and the game on the screen.

"Got a sec?" I asked, trying to keep my voice casual.

He looked up, surprised to see me on a Saturday. "Hey Crystal. You're not on 'til Monday night."

Even though Rico had my personnel file with my real name, I wasn't sure he even knew it. Which was probably just as well, that way he wouldn't accidentally use it in front of customers.

"I know. I wanted to talk about maybe picking up more shifts."

He gave me a slow once-over. "You trying to make rent or running from something?"

"Does it matter?"

He grunted. "Nope, not at all. You looking to do some doubles? I've heard the girls say that's hard on their feet."

"I was thinking maybe some weekend night shifts."

He raised his eyebrows at me.

"You know I only give Friday and Saturday nights to girls who'll work the Champagne Room."

Ah, the Champagne Room. A.k.a. the "VIP Lounge," a.k.a., "the blowjob room".

I'd made enough the last six years to survive—albeit sometimes barely—and avoid working on my knees. It was bad enough grinding on some of these guys over their pants; I couldn't imagine putting their cocks in my mouth. But I knew the money would be a lot better than my Wednesday afternoon shift.

I thought about my sister's tear-stained face, Roscoe, and my mother's fingers.

I shrugged. "Whatever you've got."

He gave me a wary look. He'd been the one to hire me when I was underage and using a fake ID, so he'd known me six years. Not once had I ever shown any interest in working in the Champagne Room. "You sure about this?"

Hell no, I'm not sure.

But thanks to Daddy Dearest, I didn't have much of a choice.

I blew out a long breath before I said with far more confidence than I was feeling, "Yep."

He watched me for another beat, like he thought if he waited long enough, I'd change my mind on the spot.

I had resolved myself to my new fate of sucking dick for money and didn't flinch, so he explained, "For your safety, you'll need to tell the bouncers when you're working back there. And the club gets thirty percent of the take, including your tips."

Of course it does.

"You only take twenty percent from me now."

His sleazy grin revealed his gold incisor.

"We're like the government. The more you make the more we take."

"Lucky me."

"You can start tonight or wait until next weekend. And of course, you can start working the Champagne Room on Monday."

I wavered just long enough for him to notice.

"You don't have to make any decisions right now. Take the weekend to think about it. I'll understand if you change your mind."

"Thanks, but I'm not sure I have much of a choice."

"I don't need the details."

"I wasn't going to give them to you."

I turned to go, but his voice followed me.

"Just so you know, you won't be able to be so damn picky about who you take into the Champagne Room. Fat fucks need to get their rocks off, too. Their money's just as good as anyone else's."

Grrrreat.

I turned around and gave him a sarcastic smile along with a "thumbs up".

"Can't wait."

Chapter Four

Vivian

The October sun was low in the sky and glared off the cracked windshield of my 2003 Chevy Malibu when I climbed back behind the steering wheel. The plastic covering the passenger window fluttered in the wind where the duct tape had lost its grip weeks ago.

I jiggled the key before turning it, and the radio jumped to Spanish talk radio like it always did, no matter how many times I'd tried to reprogram it.

The check engine light glowed bright red on the dash, mocking me as usual, but today it felt more fitting than ever. Like the check engine light on my entire life had just lit up.

I didn't bother changing the radio station. Just sat there for a second having a pity party for myself. Would my life ever not be a dumpster fire? It felt like every time I got even one step ahead, something always found a way to smack me back to where I belonged.

The air blasting through the vents was cold on my bare arms, but I hardly noticed. My mind was too full of what I'd just agreed to.

Blowjobs. For money.

Six years of dancing, grinding, teasing—but never crossing that line. And now? I was about to crawl right past it on my knees. Because of my father and his debts. Because the bastards he owed didn't care he was dead, they were still collecting.

My phone buzzed in quick bursts from inside my purse. I opened my screen to find a string of messages from my sister.

Hope: Thanks again for helping us.

Hope: Mom said to tell you thanks, too. She actually teared up.

Hope: I know you didn't have to do this. We're both really grateful.

Helping them felt right, but *how* I'd agreed to help didn't. And I already knew whatever I made wasn't going to be enough.

I stared at my wrist as my hands rested on the steering wheel. I'd gotten the phoenix tattoo to remind myself I was a survivor. It was time to prove it again. I'd find a way, whatever it took. I'd clean up Dad's shit from the grave.

My phone was still in my hand. Hope's messages were gone from the screen, but they might as well have been etched into my brain.

Champagne Room money wasn't going to cut it. Not for long. I needed more than stopgap money if I wanted to keep my family permanently safe. I needed something big. And fast.

And I knew exactly who to ask.

I opened a new text to Kit and typed before I could lose my nerve.

Me: What would I have to do to get in on one of those auctions at your club?

Chapter Five

Vivian

The front door to Velvet Underground was locked when I arrived, which I expected since the club was closed until later that evening.

I rang the bell, then looked up at the security camera with the blinking red light. Soon, the heavy door clicked, and I pushed it open to step inside.

The club looked different with the lights turned up. The sheen of the dark wood and gold trim didn't have the same nighttime allure without the soft lighting.

There was a cleaning crew in the main area that barely acknowledged me as they vacuumed and polished. I was just about to ask if they knew where I could find someone named Macy, when a lady stepped out from the hallway that, according to the placard on the wall, led to the administrative wing.

"Vivian?"

"That's me," I replied with a tone that was way more chipper than how I was feeling.

She stepped forward and offered her hand. "Hi, I'm Macy. We spoke on the phone."

Her thick brown hair with blonde highlights fell in waves across her shoulders. She was taller than me, which wasn't hard with my five-foot-three frame, but in her high heels and me in my flat sandals, she almost towered over me. Her cheekbones were sharp, thanks to an A+ contouring job, and the rest of her makeup was perfect on her flawless skin. She clutched a black tablet to her chest, almost like a clipboard.

It wasn't hard to picture her in charge of things, and I bet men tripped over themselves to help her if she needed it.

"It's nice to meet you," I said as I shook her soft hand.

Her gaze swept up and down my body, assessing me. There was nothing subtle about it.

I must have passed the first step because she motioned with her head toward the hall she'd just come from. "Let's go to my office so we can chat a little more."

Her heels clicked as she strutted down the hall, and I had to hustle to keep up with her.

"So, you're interested in being a part of the club's vendue on Friday. Do you have experience with these kinds of arrangements?"

"I'm assuming vendue means auction? If so, then yes, I'm interested, but no, I don't have specific experience with this kind of thing. But I work in a gentleman's club, so I have an idea how these things work. And my friend Kit works here; she gave me a quick rundown of what to expect."

We reached a door, and she held her hand out, gesturing me inside.

"Please have a seat," she said as she sat down in her white executive chair behind her fancy white desk with fluting around the base. It probably cost more than my car had when I bought it seven years ago.

I sat in a white leather club chair opposite her.

Most of the office was stark white, but there were pink accent pieces throughout—a vase, a throw pillow, the art on the walls. No question, this was a woman's office. I kind of loved that she maintained a feminine touch while still being no-nonsense.

"Like I told you on the phone, the club takes forty percent of the winning bid. We keep that, no matter what, and the members are aware of this. You, however, don't get paid until the contract is fulfilled. So, if you decide to void it before the term is up—which is perfectly within your purview—you walk away with nothing."

"What if the member voids it?"

"Then we'll prorate it based on the percentage of completion. But that hasn't happened in the ten years I've been working here."

I nodded.

Macy's posture was ramrod straight in her chair. "Before I explain how we ensure your safety, let me start by saying there has never been an issue in the club's almost hundred-year history. We vet our members even more than we'll vet you."

So, they're going to do a background check on me.

Although I had nothing to hide, the idea made me nervous. It just felt so *intrusive*. But I understood the need for it.

Macy continued, "We have quite a few ways we keep you safe. For starters, you'll wear a biometric bracelet from the moment you leave your house until you arrive back home and have checked in with our staff. This will be monitored remotely, but it has GPS tracking.

"Your safe word *instantly* ends any scenario, and you'll create a list of boundaries the purchasers will be made aware of before they even bid on your date."

I nodded and swallowed hard. The whole thing felt surreal. Here this beautiful, professional woman was explaining ways I'd be kept safe *once I sold myself.*

Although, I had to admit, their precautions made me a lot more comfortable with the idea of going through with this.

"That's good to know," I said in a quiet voice.

"So, you need to decide what you're offering."

I cocked my head in confusion. I thought it was obvious.

"Other than what kind of sex you're willing to do and your hard limits, you'll need to decide the length of the contract. Are you good with spending the night with your buyer? Do you want to share meals? That kind of thing."

Uhhhh.

I must have had a deer-in-the-headlights look on my face because her tone softened.

"Here's a few pointers: the more you're willing to do in the bedroom, the higher the bid is going to be. The longer the contract term, the higher the bid will be."

"How long are we talking?"

She shrugged. "I've seen women offer nothing more than a night, while the highest bid we've ever had came from someone who committed to a month."

I liked the idea of a higher price.

"But what if I'm only available Friday through Sunday?"

"Then offer a month—or however long you want—of weekends."

Was it really that simple?

It must have been, because after Macy assisted me in designing a package that would help me *sell myself for the highest price,* I walked out the door so I could be on time for my shift at Club Allure.

Hopefully Rico meant what he'd said and would understand that I'd changed my mind.

Although, I was basically doing the same thing as I'd do in the Champagne Room, at least I'd get paid better. And it'd only be for a month.

Chapter Six

Vivian

There was a knock on my apartment door just as I finished toweling off my wet hair.

I pulled my threadbare, pink terrycloth robe tighter around me, then shuffled over in my matching pink, fuzzy slippers to look through the peephole. I saw Kit standing in the hallway, so I quickly opened the door to find her holding a takeout bag in one hand and an iced coffee in the other.

She greeted me with, "You looked like you were about to throw up last time I saw you. I figured you'd have a better shot at *not* doing that if you had something in your stomach," then shoved the bag into my hands.

"Is this—?"

"Chicken shawarma plate. Rice, extra hummus. You're welcome." She breezed past me like she lived there. "And before you ask, yes, it's from the good place. I wouldn't cheap out on you at a time like this."

I followed her inside and set the food on the counter.

"You didn't have to—"

"I *wanted* to," she cut in. "Also, if you vomit onstage, I'll have to quit the club and change my name, so this is really for my benefit."

I snorted and pulled the container from the bag, then grabbed a fork.

She leaned back against the kitchen counter and watched as I took the plastic lid off. "Nervous?"

I nodded as I took a bite.

"On a scale of one to projectile?"

I shrugged as I swallowed, then cheekily replied with a grin, "Guess we'll find out soon enough."

Her expression softened, and she grabbed my wrist. "You've got this, Viv. You're the baddest bitch I know."

Then her thumb pressed against my tattoo. "Seriously. You're going full-on *Pretty Woman* to keep *fucking loan sharks* from chopping off your mom's fingers. That's so badass. And kind of heroic. In a slutty, high-end-escort kind of way."

I laughed, even as the chicken shawarma felt stuck in my throat. "That's me. Slutty and heroic."

"You're gonna blow them away." She smirked. "Hopefully not literally, unless they pay for that."

I rolled my eyes, but the laugh helped. Kit always knew how to pull me back from the edge.

She nudged my shoulder. "Finish eating. Then we're picking out what you're wearing tonight. You're not getting auctioned off looking like a hot mess."

I took another bite, still nervous as fuck, but steadier than before.

I could do this. I *would* do this.

It was my only option.

CHAPTER SEVEN

Vivian

The dressing room at Velvet Underground was a flurry of activity when I walked in. Beautiful women in various stages of getting ready—some wielded curling irons or lipstick tubes, while others were busy adjusting tit tape or fluffing their hair. The scents of perfume and hairspray hung in the air.

The energy and smells felt a lot like the dressing room at Club Allure, and I welcomed the familiarity.

There were marked differences from the strip club, however. The couches around the room were plush and inviting instead of being stained, threadbare petri dishes no one wanted to touch. The mirrors lining the back of the room were all sparkling clean and flake-free, and the light bulbs in the mirrors at the makeup stations all worked.

I hung the wardrobe bag with my auction outfit on a rolling garment rack, and dropped my other one, packed for the weekend, onto the floor. Macy had been clear: I wouldn't be going home until Sunday. Hopefully, I'd come back with my dignity intact and not full of regret I couldn't scrub off in the shower.

A few of the women looked like they belonged in magazines. One raven-haired beauty lay inverted on a couch while scrolling through her phone. She was clad in a purple silk robe and black thigh-high nylons; her legs stuck in the air like she hadn't a care in the world. Another dark-haired woman hummed while she applied lip gloss, while a siren with auburn hair was doing a tree pose in her bra and panties next to her makeup table. They all seemed so calm, so used to this.

Me? I was still deciding if my outfit said *elegant and fuckable* or *goodwill and desperate*.

I unzipped the bag and pulled out the red dress Kit had helped me pick out earlier. With a deep breath, I thought, "Here goes nothing."

~~~~

I stood in front of the mirror to inspect my appearance and nervously tugged at the hem of the clingy fabric on my dress. It hugged my waist and hips and revealed enough cleavage to be considered scandalous in any other setting than a sex club. Kit had said the thigh slit made the dress, "Elegantly slutty."

"Is that a nice way to say trashy?"

"Absolutely not. That dress is going to make a statement."

"What? That I'm trying to ball on a budget?"

"Sweets, the way you're going to look in that dress, the only balls those men will be thinking about are theirs as you drain them."

I'd let out a sigh and hung the dress in the garment bag before putting a pair of red come-fuck-me shoes I wore at work in the bottom. "Yeah."

"Don't get in your head about this. It's not like you haven't hooked up with randos before, but bonus, you're getting paid to do it this time. And maybe you'll get a few orgasms out of the deal, too."

Which was more than I could say for the last guy I'd gone home with from the bar.

"You're right. I can do this. Hell, I shake my tits onstage on a regular basis."

But I'd never taken money for actual sex. I'd worried that once I crossed the line, it'd be easy to do it again. Which was why I'd resisted doing it, even when my rent had been overdue.

But this was different. This was my family's safety. And I'd cross the line for them.

The gorgeous woman who'd been doing the tree pose earlier glanced over at me with a warm smile. "You clean up nice, Blondie."

"Thanks. First time," I admitted.

"Welcome to the circus." She held out a manicured hand. "I'm Cherry."

"Shit, was I supposed to give a stage name?"

I hadn't thought about that, and Macy hadn't mentioned it.

Even Cherry's laugh was sexy.

"No, believe it or not, that's my real name. I think my parents were sealing my fate from the get-go."

"Did you get teased a lot growing up?"

"Not too bad in elementary and middle, but by the time high school came around and I developed tits and guys only thought with their dicks..." She got a far-off look in her eyes and murmured, "Yeah, that was tough."

She was quiet for a beat, then like the spell was broken, she looked back at me with a smile. "And now I manipulate men with sex and make six figures doing it."

"That's a great way to look at it."

It was the same attitude I took at the club when guys were peeling off fifties and hundreds so I'd come talk to them and sit on their laps.

She touched my arm. "You're going to be fine. The members here are kinky fucks, some more than others, but at least at the end of the day, you don't have to worry you're going to be cut up in little pieces and dumped in the ocean. Instead, you're going to have a fat stack of cash."

"That's what I'm here for."

She gave me a wink. "Aren't we all, honey."

~~~~

I zipped my overnight bag and slid it under the dressing bench just as Kit walked in.

"Damn, look at you." She gave me an approving nod. "Total smoke show. I knew that dress was the one. You're going to knock 'em dead."

I smiled, although I wasn't as convinced. The women here were super nice, but they were way out of my league. "I'm glad you think so." I made a point of looking around. "I'm worried they're going to take one look at me and wonder who allowed the discount date in the lineup."

Kit rolled her eyes. "Stop it, you're gorgeous," then pulled a travel-size bottle of vodka from her purse and handed it to me, saying, "You obviously could use a little liquid courage."

"I mean, you're not wrong," I quipped as I unscrewed the top and took a swig.

Macy appeared in the doorway wearing an all-cream pantsuit that fit her like a glove with matching pointy-toed pumps. It was understated but conveyed she was not only beautiful but also in charge.

"You ladies look amazing! Are you ready?" she asked, glancing down at the tablet in her hand.

There was a chorus of, "Yes" and a few, "Almost," while last-minute touches to their makeup and hair were made.

I let out a cleansing breath with a hand on my stomach and murmured, "Yeah," even though I wasn't so sure anymore.

Macy gave me a once-over. "You look great. They're going to love you," she said, then pointed to the woman who'd had her legs in the air just an hour earlier. "Nadia—we're starting in five, and you're up first."

Nadia, who looked like she could walk the Red Carpet in her black evening gown and stilettos, fluffed her hair in the mirror as she assured Macy, "I'm ready."

Macy then glanced at her tablet and rattled off the order the ten women in the room would appear onstage. I was third.

At least I'd get it over with instead of pacing in the dressing room.

Nadia followed Macy out, and a few minutes later, a man's muffled voice made it backstage.

"Good evening, gentlemen. Welcome to October's vendue. We have ten stunning women offering packages that I think will satisfy all of you kinky bastards." The man chuckled, then followed up with, "Well, most of you, anyway," which garnered laughter from the crowd before he continued, "So without further ado, I'll turn the microphone over to tonight's emcee, Velvet Underground's very own Macy Chambers."

Macy's voice was strong over the speakers when she introduced Nadia, and seconds later, a woman with a headset, dressed in black yoga pants and black t-shirt, appeared in the doorway of the dressing room and called out, "Sidney, you're on deck!"

A blonde bombshell in a teal dress that was cut down to her navel stood up and strutted out.

I swallowed hard and turned back to the mirror for one last look. Kit gave my hand a squeeze.

"You've got this. It's just like you're going onstage at the club."

Yeah, except instead of sitting on a man's lap and bouncing my tits in his face when my dance was through, I'd be spreading my legs in his house or at a hotel, depending on if he was married or not.

Macy's voice over the speakers exclaimed, "We have a winning bid!" That made what I was about to do even more real, and I realized there was no turning back.

I hope I earned enough tonight to make this worth it.

Chapter Eight

Jeff

I didn't come here to spend money.

I came for the scotch and a place to unwind after three nights doing my ER rotation. The vendue nights—just fucking call it an auction, already—were always entertaining, half soft-core fantasy, half financial dick-measuring contest. Most of the time, I just observed. I didn't need to shell out money to get laid.

Tonight should've been no different.

I slid into a seat in one of the private booths angled toward the stage near the center, and nodded when the girl in the tight blouse with the top three buttons undone asked, "Macallan, sir?"

The man beside me nodded. "Jeff, good to see you again."

"Bradford," I replied. "I didn't know you came to these things."

He chuckled. "Normally I don't. But my wife's in Europe for another few weeks, so I thought maybe I'd see if the tight piece of ass I hooked up with at the masquerade ball was up for sale."

"But how will you know if it's her? Wasn't she wearing a mask? And every chick onstage is a hot piece of ass."

He smiled knowingly. "I'll know. She had a tattoo on her wrist."

I was careful to school my expression and took a sip of my single malt scotch before I responded.

"Oh yeah? Don't tell me, a Bible verse? Chinese symbol?"

"No... well, maybe? Is a phoenix considered a Chinese symbol?"

Fuck. Me.

Phoenix hooked up with *Bradford*? Like he'd been a better alternative than *me*?

I drawled in response, "I think it's from the Greek."

He went on, chuckling to himself. "She hopped on my cock and rode me like a cowgirl. Her cunt was nice and tight, and so was her ass."

My eyebrows went up. "You fucked her ass?"

"No, just squeezed it when I blasted my load in her." He adjusted in his seat. "Damn, I'm getting a chub just thinking about it."

My smile was purposefully condescending. "Well, maybe you'll get lucky, and she'll be here tonight, and you can continue where you left off."

For her sake, she better not be. Because Bradford sure as hell wouldn't have the winning bid, and I'd make damn certain she regretted ever putting herself up for sale.

Macy's voice rang out.

"And now, number three on tonight's vendue list—Vivian."

I noticed the red dress first. Then the hair. Then the eyes.

My glass hit the table harder than I meant it to.

So, Phoenix's real name was Vivian.

I said it to myself a few times to see how it felt.

Yeah, it suited her.

Bradford leaned forward with interest. "Oh, hell yes! That's her." He rubbed his hands together with glee. "Looks like I'm going to be having some fun for a few weeks."

Yeah, sorry, buddy. Not with her, you're not.

She strutted across the stage like she owned the club, but she had a few tells that let me know she wasn't as confident as she pretended to be. The tightness in her shoulders, the way her eyes darted around the room. Underneath her painted-on confidence, there was a vulnerability.

One that I was going to exploit until she broke.

She'd turned me down. Then fucked *Bradford*. Had she fucked that frat douche, too?

And now she was selling herself? To anyone?

Grayson made the initial bid, quickly followed by Bradford's counter bid.

Bid all you want assholes, it ain't happenin'.

I sat up straighter, my jaw locked and heart pounding harder than I'd like to admit.

Let's play, sweetheart.

Let's see what you're worth.

~~~~

After Grayson made the first move, Bradford jumped in like a dog chasing a bone. Then some other guy threw in a bid to show he could. And just like that, a dick-measuring contest began.

Macy clearly loved it; her voice oozed satisfaction as she paced the stage. "Gentlemen, let me remind you what's being offered. This package includes *four weekends—Friday through Sunday—of her time.* Hard limits have been submitted and must be honored: *no pain, no waterplay, full respect for the safe word.*"

She gave the crowd a sly smile. "And this is her *first appearance* on our stage. A virgin, if you will. Completely untouched by any previous arrangement."

Bradford snorted. "Well, not *completely* untouched."

I'd never wanted to throat-punch someone more.

But Macy's words worked. The men perked up and bids rose fast.

Forty thousand. Forty-five. Fifty.

Bradford shifted uncomfortably in his seat. I couldn't help but smirk thinking that we were getting into the range where he might have a hard time explaining to his wife where that money went.

Fifty-five. Fifty-seven. Sixty.

I didn't even realize I was standing until I was already on my feet and declared, "One hundred thousand."

The room snapped silent.

Macy's brows lifted, but she recovered quickly. "We have a new high bid of one hundred thousand. Do I hear one hundred and five?"

I looked around the room, silently daring anyone to go higher.

Not because I wanted her. Not because she was special.

Because she'd turned me down and given herself to someone else.

And now, she was mine to punish for doing just that.

No one moved.

I didn't sit. I didn't blink. I locked eyes with Vivian.

She froze and her eyes went wide for a breath, then her chin tipped up defiantly, like I'd seen before.

Bradford leaned toward me and muttered under his breath, "Fucking asshole."

I didn't respond; didn't even look at him. Let the fucker seethe. He wasn't worth a reply.

The adrenaline had drowned out everything but her.

The dress. The eyes. That look she gave me like she wasn't sure if she wanted to run or fight.

Oh, choose fight, baby girl. Please. That will be fun.

She had no business putting herself up for sale to the highest bidder after giving Bradford what should've been mine. And now I got to erase him from her—one brutal, filthy inch at a time.

Time to pay the piper, sweetheart.

You get to serve the man you thought wasn't good enough to fuck for free.

I own you now—your body, your obedience, your tears, your shame. I'm going to make you crawl for every goddamn cent like the good little whore you chose to be.

And when it's over, you'll beg me to take more. And hate yourself for doing it.

****

Vivian

I was pleasantly surprised when I heard the bids climbing. I'd had myself half-convinced before I went onstage that I'd be lucky if my "package" sold for a thousand dollars. Then a deep voice offered one hundred thousand.

After the club took their forty percent, that would leave me with sixty.

Sixty *thousand* dollars. That was enough to put a real dent in Daddy Dearest's debt. Maybe enough that we could actually pay it off before the interest ate up any progress we made.

My mom, sister, and Roscoe would be safe.

It was way more than I'd been expecting. More than I thought I'd ever be worth.

But it came with a price and the reality of what that price was sat like a pit in my stomach.

I'd just sold myself.

Four weekends of sex. Whatever was in the fine print that didn't count as physical pain. Whatever the buyer wanted, as long as it wasn't against the rules.

But there was no going back now. That was too much money to walk away from. Not when my family needed it.

I held my head high and kept my face still.

I could survive this. I could survive anything; I even had the tattoo on my wrist to remind me of that.

Macy's voice echoed from the stage speakers. "Sold for one hundred thousand dollars to Dr. Jeff Connolly."

My heart lodged in my throat.

Dr. Connolly.

I blinked. It couldn't be him. It had to be someone else. Someone with the same name.

But then I saw him, standing next to the center booth near the stage, looking as if he didn't have a care in the world. He'd been wearing a mask at the ball, but there was no mistaking those blue eyes belonged to the man I'd turned down that evening. The blue eyes that had locked on mine. Blue orbs that were now staring right through me like he owned me.

Which, technically, he did. For the next four weekends anyway.

I forced myself to take a deep breath as I tried to make sense of what was going on.

He hadn't chosen me before. He'd walked away like I wasn't worth the trouble.

And now he'd paid one hundred grand to own me for a month.

Why now?

I couldn't shake the feeling that this was personal.

What I didn't know was why.

Chapter Nine

Vivian

I stepped backstage on shaky legs, barely aware of the applause that met me in the dressing room.

Voices buzzed around me—compliments, questions, a few playful jabs—but it all sounded muffled, like I was underwater. My blood still thrummed in my ears, drowning everything else out.

"Damn, a hundred grand?"

"She must've offered something real dirty in her little weekend package."

"I mean, she looked hot. I would've bid on her."

"Guess I need to step up my game."

Cherry touched my arm, offering a grin. "You okay, Blondie?"

I nodded. Or maybe I didn't. I wasn't sure. Everything felt surreal.

I sank into one of the couches near the makeup station I'd used earlier where my weekend bag still sat. My fingers fidgeted in my lap while I tried to focus on anything—my breathing, the feel of the seat under me, the ticking of the clock on the wall—but nothing helped.

Dr. Connolly. The one who'd walked away so easily had just paid one hundred thousand dollars for me.

Why?

Somewhere, ladies giggled nervously as they said goodbye to one another. The auction continued. More girls came back into the room and left. I lost count.

Then Macy's heels clicked toward me, crisp and unmistakable. I hadn't even noticed the stage had gone quiet.

She stopped in front of me and leaned in, her voice low. "He asked for you."

I looked up. "Now?"

Her mouth tightened. "You don't say no. Not to him. And definitely not after that number."

I gave a small nod. There was no avoiding it—time to deliver what I'd sold.

"He's waiting in the main room."

****

Jeff

Bradford moved to a table near the bar, all smugness gone. He kept glancing over his shoulder like he wanted to say something but knew better. Felix Alvarez, still in his three-piece suit to remind everyone how much he worked, leaned in to talk to Bradford. Hopefully to ask if Bradford's balls had finally dropped out of his stomach after getting outbid that hard. Probably not, though. More than likely, it was to position himself so Bradford would feel comfortable asking for a favor someday, then he'd owe Alvarez. Which was exactly what the dude wanted.

That was the thing about this place—it wasn't just about sex. It was politics. Leverage. Power. Favors.

A glass clinked gently on my table.

"I'll admit," came a voice to my left, "I didn't see that coming."

I turned as Grayson slid into the booth beside me. He was dressed casually tonight, same as me. Except he'd paired his Levi's with a light-blue cashmere sweater instead of the navy button-down I had on.

He raised his drink. "A hundred grand's a hell of a statement."

I shrugged. "Hopefully she's worth it."

Grayson studied me for a beat; his relaxed smile didn't reach his eyes. "I hope so, too. For your sake." He took another sip of scotch before adding, "She didn't look like she belonged up there."

"That's because she didn't."

He gave a slow nod. "She's either going to break... or beg."

I didn't blink. "She'll do both."

The corner of his mouth tipped up in... respect?

"Have fun breaking her. Just be careful she doesn't break you first." He paused as he slid to the edge of the booth, then added with a heartless smile, "Though if she does, I'd be happy to take a turn. Ruining pretty things is kind of what I do."

I didn't respond, just stared back at him. I'd heard that Grayson could be as big a bastard as me. His words seemed to confirm the rumors.

He gave a lazy nod, then stood and disappeared into the crowd.

Now that the auction was over, the energy in the room had shifted.

Some of the auctioned women were already cozying up to their new owners—settling into laps, whispering into ears, tits pressed against arms. Others hovered nearby, laughing too loudly or gazing up like the man had cured cancer. It was all an act, but if the men noticed, they didn't care. They played along, clinking their champagne flutes like it was the start of a decadent honeymoon.

Eyes flicked toward me now and then. Curious. No one said it, but I could feel the question hanging in the air: *Why her? Why that price?*

They were waiting for fireworks.

And they were about to get them.

I faltered with my second glass of Macallan halfway to my mouth when I saw her.

She was as fucking beautiful as the night I'd first seen her. But instead of looking like an angel in white, she was now the devil in red.

I loosened my cuffs and rolled up my sleeves.

Time to collect.

Her eyes skated around the room as she walked toward me, like she was searching for exits. Or allies.

Sorry, sweetheart. There's no one coming to save you.

When she reached my table, I didn't say a word, just pointed to the surface of it and ordered, "Up."

****

Vivian

My feet stopped when I reached his table. He didn't greet me. Didn't ask how I was or offer me a drink.

He just pointed at the table like I was a dog and gave me the command of, "Up."

I hated myself for how quickly I scrambled to obey.

I perched my bottom on the tabletop, careful to keep my knees together as he spun me until I was situated directly in front of him. I could feel the room's collective breath being held as they watched and waited to see what happened next.

Jeff didn't look at me after that. Just leaned back and surveyed the room while he sipped his scotch and pretended I wasn't even there.

Finally, his eyes dragged up my body, unhurried and callous.

"Spread your legs."

My breath caught.

He draped one arm over the backrest like he had all the time in the world. "Don't make me tell you again."

My body tensed. Every cell screamed *no*. But between my thighs, I was soaked—humiliated and dripping wet. And I knew he was about to find out.

I lifted my bum to hike my dress higher around my thighs, then parted my legs.

He grinned in satisfaction.

"Such a good whore," he murmured as he traced a finger down my seam. "Already putting on a show for your new owner. Look how wet your cunt is for me."

Men's laughter, low, and appreciative, rippled from the nearby tables.

"Look how fucking soaked she is," someone said.

"That's a damn good whore right there."

"I'll bet she'll be worth every dollar," while still another crudely asked, "Is she tight, Doc?"

Jeff's smile was cruel when he shoved two fingers inside me and chucked darkly, "Oh yeah. But not for long," before adding a third, then a fourth.

The peanut gallery cackled in delight. "Yeah. Break that bitch."

"Use that cunt up. You paid for it."

"Can you make her squirt?"

Jeff tilted his head and replied, "Hmm, I don't know." He directed his attention to me. "Do you squirt, whore?"

He didn't wait for me to reply, just gave an evil grin and said, "Let's find out, shall we?"

The men whooped and hollered in agreement.

I clenched my stomach, trying to fight my arousal, but every filthy word, every vulgar comment from the crowd only turned me on more.

My thighs trembled, my face flushed, and I hated that I couldn't stop the slick drip between my legs—or the way my pussy greedily grasped his fingers.

I wanted to come. God, I was *desperate* for it. But I knew the second I did, it would seal my place in his eyes. Not just his bought whore, but a slut who loved performing for an audience.

My hands sought for purchase against the slick table, to no avail, as I tried to hold on to something—anything—to try to stop my body from responding while he played it like his personal violin. His fingers curled and pumped with ruthless precision, pressing right where he knew I couldn't ignore it.

Pressure built fast, and I began to pant.

Then I felt it—hot and sudden, pulsing out of me in a helpless gush.

I hadn't come.

But my body had given him something else.

The crowd erupted.

"Fuck yes!"

"She *squirted*—look at that slut drip!"

"Didn't even get her off, and she made a mess. What a filthy whore."

"That's a fun toy you just bought yourself, Jeff."

My heart slammed in my chest, but it wasn't just mortification that made it hard to breathe.

It was the awful, aching truth:

I *liked* it.

****

Jeff

She squirted. Everywhere.

It splashed onto the table, onto my shirt cuff, and dripped down her thighs. And the room went *feral*.

Fucking perfect.

They all saw it, that her body belonged to me now. Not just because I paid. Because I knew exactly how to use her.

Laughter. Crude praise. More bets about what I could make her do next. But I wasn't listening to them anymore.

I was watching *her*.

Eyes glazed. Lips parted. Her whole body shook as she tried to hold back the inevitable.

But I wasn't going to let her.

"Still holding on?" I murmured, dragging my soaked fingers down her inner thigh, then up again, pressing ruthlessly against her clit.

She whimpered, eyes fluttering shut.

"No," I snapped. "Eyes on me."

They opened. Wide. Frightened. *Fascinated.*

"Everyone's watching, sweetheart," I reminded her. "You gonna make a pretty little 'O' face when you come for me?"

She tried to shake her head.

I gave her clit one sharp slap and demanded, "Lie back!"

She cried out, and then did as she was told. My fingers were on her again, rubbing hard and fast. No teasing now. No mercy.

I watched her fight it. The way her hands clawed at the table. The trembling in her thighs. The desperation not to give in and the way it broke when she did.

She came *hard*, gasping my name like a curse.

Her hips jerked, and her cunt spasmed around nothing. My cock strained against my zipper, desperate to fill the hole she just proved she needed me in.

I smiled. Slow. Cruel.

"There it is," I said, loud enough for the whole room to hear. "Now say thank you, whore."

She didn't respond fast enough, so I slapped her sensitive clit until she cried out, "Thank you!"

The applause was thunderous.

She just lay there; shaking, soaked, ruined.

Exactly how I wanted her.

Exactly how she was supposed to be.

Mine.

Chapter Ten

Jeff

She refused to look at me as the chauffeured car the club had provided me pulled away from Velvet Underground.

Good.

Her mascara was smudged, and her thighs were still slick with her own arousal and squirt. She'd tried wiping it off but I'd stopped her.

I stretched one arm across the back of the seat and let the silence hang heavy in the air.

Leaning over, I demanded, "Show me your pussy."

Finally, her gaze snapped to mine. Her eyes widened then she glanced at the rearview mirror. She knew the driver could see.

I couldn't help but grin with sadistic glee.

Yeah, exactly. That's the point.

She waffled, just long enough to amuse me, then with resignation to her fate, shifted forward on the seat and hiked up the hem of her dress so she could properly part her legs.

Outside the tinted window, the city rolled by.

Inside, I stared down at the wet, glistening mess between her thighs and felt my cock twitch in approval.

"Look at this, Tom." I spread her open with one hand then dragged my fingers through her slick folds with the other. She shuddered at my touch. "She's still soaked. I think she likes showing you her cunt."

The driver's eyes wavered between the mirror and the road. I could see the grin on his face, but he didn't say anything, so I kept going. "You should have seen it. She squirted all over the table in front of everyone."

Tom's chuckle was low. "I'll bet that was a helluva sight."

I plunged two fingers inside her, and she tilted her hips slightly. I wasn't even sure if she was aware she'd done it. The sound of her arousal echoed off the cab of the car as I finger fucked her.

"Then she came for them, too." I brushed my lips against her ear and murmured, "You loved putting on a show, didn't you whore? Just like you love letting Tom watch."

"No," she whimpered.

"Lying slut." I dragged my soaked fingers out and held them up. "Look how wet she is, Tom."

"I think she likes it, sir."

I wiped my fingers across her mouth. "Yeah. She does."

Vivian's legs trembled, still spread wide.

"You want to come again, don't you?"

"No."

I chuckled as I circled her clit, and she bit her lip to hold back a moan.

"Liar."

I directed my comments to the driver but kept my eyes on Vivian's face. "What do you think, Tom? Should I let her come?"

"If you think she's earned it, sir."

That's exactly what I wanted to hear.

I pulled my hand away and she whimpered at the loss. "She definitely has *not* earned it."

Reaching forward, I pressed the button, and the divider slid up with a mechanical hum, sealing us off.

"But I have."

I unzipped and pulled out my cock, thick and aching.

"Get to work, whore."

****

Vivian

I stared at him, and for one insane second, I considered saying no.

But then I remembered the price tag he'd slapped on me. One hundred thousand dollars. He owned me. And this was what I'd agreed to.

I slid off the seat and sank to my knees on the floorboard, the carpet rough beneath my skin. I wrapped my fingers around his thick length. The tip dripped precum, and I smeared it around the crown with my thumb as I looked up at him.

His eyes were cold as he watched me swirl my tongue around the head, tasting his salty tanginess. His musk filled my senses. I took a deep breath to savor his scent, before pulling him deeper into my mouth. I hollowed my cheeks and sucked gently, trying to find a rhythm, but my own arousal still pulsed between my legs, distracting me.

"Deeper," he said, voice calm but ruthless. "I want you to choke on it."

I did as he said, opening my throat and sliding my mouth down until my nose brushed his stomach. My eyes watered, and he groaned when I looked up at him.

"Fuck yes," he snarled as his hand came down on the back of my head and fisted my hair. "Just like that."

He thrust up as he pressed my head down. His tip hit the back of my throat with each push.

"Keep sucking, slut."

I knew every name he called me was meant to degrade me and remind me what I'd become. But all they did was make me wet. He was right—I was a whore.

Tears slipped from the corners of my eyes, but I didn't stop. I couldn't. I wanted to hate him. But I found I wanted to please him more.

He groaned again and held my head tight against him. "You going to swallow like a good little cumdump, or do I need to paint your face for the driver to see when we pull up?"

I whimpered around him, and he laughed triumphantly. The sound was dark and mean.

Then he held my head and grunted as his hot cum hit the back of my throat.

"Take it all," he snarled through gritted teeth. "Don't spill a fucking drop."

I swallowed it all, and pulled my mouth off his cock, leaving his shaft spit shined.

He looked down at me, his thumb sweeping gently along the corner of my mouth.

"Good girl," he murmured, quieter this time. Almost... reverently.

Chapter Eleven

Vivian

The car turned onto a long, winding drive lined with soft lights, and my breath caught when Jeff's house came into view. It wasn't just big—it was beautiful. Two stories of warm stone and wood, with golden lights glowing through tall windows. The kind of place my mom used to drive me and Hope by at Christmas time, and I'd imagine myself living in one day. The kind of place where things were quiet and safe.

It was nothing like my cramped studio apartment. Or the house I grew up in, where the walls were stained with cigarette smoke and the windows rattled in their frames when my father yelled.

It was picture-perfect, and not at all where I belonged.

The car rolled to a stop. Tom opened the rear door and his face split into a knowing grin when his eyes flicked to my rumpled dress and bare thighs as he helped me out. I didn't meet his gaze. Jeff stepped out next and turned to wait for Tom to retrieve my bag from the trunk.

Once he had it, I reached for the handle, but Jeff shook his head. "I've got it."

That surprised me, but I didn't say anything as I followed him up the stone path to the grand, double-door mahogany entrance.

He opened the front door and gestured me inside.

I stepped past him and tried not to gawk at the ornate chandelier hanging from the high ceiling in the foyer. The floors looked like hardwood but sounded like tile as my stilettos clicked over the planks. The smell of mahogany and leather filled the air.

The door shut behind me, followed by the quiet clunk of a lock. I turned toward the sound.

Jeff moved past me, setting my bag down next to a table in the entryway, then pulled a small velvet box from the inside pocket of his wool jacket.

"Come here."

I obeyed, and he opened the lid to reveal a black leather choker with a slim silver O-ring at the center which made its purpose clear.

He lifted the collar from the box, placed it around my neck, then fastened it in the back.

"This stays on until your contract ends. You can take it off to shower, but that's it. If I find it off any other time, we're done."

"Even during the week when I'm not here?"

"*Especially* during the week."

I swallowed and nodded.

"Rules," he said. "You speak when spoken to. You don't sit on furniture unless I've told you it's allowed. You don't touch yourself unless I tell you to. You're not to come unless I've given you permission. Your holes will be available to me at all times." He gave me a pointed look. "*All* of them. That means you'll either be naked, in a dress, or a t-shirt without panties. Got it?"

Another nod. I couldn't have found my voice if I tried.

"You'll sleep naked in the guest room down the hall from me. If I want you during the night, I'll come get you."

He tilted my chin up. "Basically, you're a warm hole with manners."

My breath caught, but I didn't argue. A hundred thousand dollars gave him the right to make these demands.

"Strip."

I moved to kick my red stilettos off, but he shook his head. "The heels stay on."

I reached behind me and tugged the zipper down, then let the fabric pool at my feet before stepping out of it.

He walked around me, appraising my body with his stare. I didn't wilt as I stood there. This wasn't my first rodeo. Men did that shit to me nightly.

Finally, he nodded once, then said, "You'll do. Let's take the tour," before heading down the hall without looking to see if I was following him.

He moved quickly, and I had to practically jog to keep up, which was no easy feat when you're naked and in four-inch heels. We passed through the kitchen, the library, the gym, and the den. All of it was beautiful with dark wood and masculine decor. I wished I'd had time to stop and admire it.

But it was obvious I wasn't here to appreciate the craftsmanship of his home.

When we reached the upstairs landing, he stopped.

"Hands on the railing. Ass out. Eyes forward."

I assumed the position and gripped the wood with both hands.

I heard his zipper go down, then he gripped my hips and thrust his cock inside my pussy. No checking if I was wet and ready, no warning. No kindness. Just raw possession.

I moaned softly.

"Stay quiet."

He drove into me over and over, every thrust made my tits bounce and the collar jingle softly around my throat.

His grunts grew louder and finally he gave one last thrust before snarling, "That's it, whore. Take it," as I felt rope after rope of his cum fill me.

He stayed seated inside me while he caught his breath, then pulled out and spun me around, then pushed me to my knees.

"Clean it."

I pulled him into my mouth and the tanginess of his cum mixed with my pussy juices hit my tongue.

"Do you taste your cunt?"

I assumed it was a rhetorical question and continued cleaning his dick off without replying.

Finally, he pushed me off, so I landed on my ass while he zipped up.

"Your room's at the end of the hall on the right." He took a couple of steps, then threw a warning over his shoulder. "And don't even think about touching that pussy. It belongs to me now."

Then he walked down the hall and disappeared into a room, leaving me on my ass with his cum dripping out of my pussy and onto the floor.

****

Jeff

I didn't look back at her when I left her on the landing. I didn't need to. Sixty thousand dollars said she wasn't going anywhere.

And I was going to make sure she earned every dollar.

I walked into my room and peeled off my shirt, followed by my jeans. My cock was still hard as I pictured how I'd left her—naked on the floor except for the stilettos and the collar I'd picked up from Macy when I paid my bill.

I hadn't planned on bidding tonight. Hell, I hadn't even planned on staying long. But the moment she stepped on that stage, I knew I had to have her.

Macy had asked if I wanted to buy a collar, too, when I'd handed her my credit card.

"It might help make the power dynamic clearer."

I'd wanted to tell her there would be no confusion about who owned her, but then I thought it might be a nice reminder when we were apart.

Seeing it around her neck now? It did something to me. I'd have to thank Macy for the suggestion next time I saw her.

I sat on the edge of the bed and scrubbed a hand down my face. The little Phoenix hadn't cried. Hadn't begged. She'd just taken everything I gave her. Let me humiliate her at the club and in the car, then strip her and parade her naked through my house before I bent her over and fucked her raw.

In fact, based on how fucking soaked she got, I dared say she liked it.

And now she was under my roof. Collared.

Mine.

My cock stirred again. I didn't even try to fight it.

I stood and headed back down the hall. The guest room door was slightly ajar, and I pushed it open without knocking.

She was curled up under the covers, her hands in a prayer pose, with her eyes closed.

I stepped into the room and shut the door behind me, then pulled the comforter off her.

"Spread your legs."

She rolled onto her back and did as I demanded without a word.

Good whore.

Maybe this time I'd even let her come.

Chapter Twelve

Vivian

The room was light when I opened my eyes, but it felt like there was something in my throat. I tried to cough, then realized it was Jeff's cock as he straddled my face. His hand fisted my hair as he guided my mouth up and down his shaft.

"Good morning, whore." He thrust so his balls rested on my chin. "I wanted you to start your day right." He lightly slapped my cheek with his free hand. "Open wide."

I did as he commanded and opened my mouth wider while relaxing my throat to allow him to slide his cock deeper inside.

"Oh yeah, that's it," he moaned as he started to increase the tempo, and I made gagging noises around the shaft. "Choke on that dick. Yeah. Just like that."

My eyes watered as his cock easily glided in and out of my mouth from how much spit I'd produced.

He grunted, and I could taste his salty precum. Then he pulled out, aiming at my face as he jerked himself off until he started to spurt, and glazed me from forehead to chin.

The corner of his mouth turned up as he looked down at me, then smeared the warm goo around my skin with the tip of his cock.

"Clean it."

I did the best I could from the angle I was lying. Finally, he pulled out and rolled off the bed.

"Get cleaned up. I'm making breakfast."

I went to the bathroom and did exactly as he instructed.

Now I sat on the cool marble island in the kitchen with my legs spread wide, just like he'd ordered when I came downstairs, as he flipped omelets at the stove. My nipples were stiff under his white t-shirt from the air conditioning. The collar jingled around my neck whenever I moved. A quiet reminder of my place here.

He hadn't said a word to me since pointing at the counter and saying, "Spread your legs. I want to see your hole."

He slid two omelets on two plates, then set them on the counter so he could run his finger down my slit, chuckling slightly as he did.

"Look how wet you are. You like being my whore." He pulled his hand away and picked up the plates. "Come sit."

I don't know what I'd been expecting, but it hadn't been that. I moved off the counter and padded to the table before he changed his mind, sitting in the chair he pulled out for me. We ate in silence. I didn't know if I was allowed to speak.

"How old are you?" he asked after a few minutes.

"Twenty-three."

"College?"

"I try to take a few courses a year. It's all I can afford, but it's still progress forward, I guess."

He nodded and kept eating. Nothing about work or what I was majoring in. Just superficial small talk, like the strangers we were.

When I stood to gather the plates, he stopped me.

"Leave it."

"Oh, okay. Are you sure? I'm happy to help clean up."

He stood and circled behind me with his hand sliding up my neck. Squeezing lightly, he murmured in my ear, "No, I've got something else in mind for you."

****

Jeff

"Up on the island."

She obeyed, climbing onto the marble surface and parting her legs without instruction. She knew better now.

I stepped back to admire the view. She was naked under one of my white t-shirts, with the overhead lights reflecting off the silver ring of her collar. The sight of her spread open, while knowing I could do anything I wanted to her, made my cock twitch.

I opened the fridge and grabbed a chilled Pellegrino bottle. Condensation coated the glass. Perfect.

Stepping back between her legs, I ran the bottle along her inner thigh and watched her shiver.

"I think this is much better than doing dishes, don't you?"

She nodded once, eyes uncertain but locked on mine.

I untwisted the cap and poured some of the contents down her seam. She gasped and flinched from the cold, fizzing water, but otherwise kept her legs spread.

Good girl.

Dumping the rest of the contents down the sink, I then dragged the bottle's neck between her folds. She tilted her hips forward in invitation, and I couldn't help but chuckle.

"Such a greedy whore."

I pressed the bottle inside her, and she arched her back with her hands braced against the edge of the counter.

My hand flexed around the glass as I eased it in another inch, then another, all the while watching her squirm.

"Still so damn tight," I said, mostly to myself. "And wet. You like being used, don't you?"

She didn't answer. She didn't need to. We both knew it was true.

I twisted the bottle slowly, grinding it against her slick walls, then withdrew it halfway out before pressing it back in again. Her breath hitched and a shiver ran through her.

I smirked as I pumped it harder.

"You like being fucked by a bottle, don't you?"

She gasped, "No," but then let out a low moan.

She didn't *want* to like being fucked by the makeshift glass dildo, but her juices on the green glass said otherwise.

If I made her come, there'd be no way she could deny it.

With a devilish grin, I rubbed her clit with one hand as I worked the water bottle in and out of her. She let out a tiny moan while her pussy greedily gripped it.

"That's it, whore. Take that bottle in your cunt."

I doubled down on my ministrations on her clit and chuckled with evil glee when her body went so tight, I could have let go of the bottle and she would have held it in place.

"You're going to come, aren't you slut? You're going to come while you're getting fucked with a bottle because you're a filthy girl."

She protested, but her body didn't agree.

"No!"

"Yeah, you are. You're going to come like a dirty whore." I rubbed her clit faster and demanded, "Say it. Say, 'I'm a dirty whore'."

Suddenly, her tight body convulsed as the orgasm racked through her, and she screamed out, "I'mmm a dirrrrrty whorrrre."

Yeah, you are.

Satisfaction rolled off me in waves as I continued pumping in and out of her until she locked her knees together.

I pulled the bottle from her pussy and put it to her lips. "Drink up," even though I knew it was empty.

Still, she lifted her head and opened her mouth in case there was something left.

"That's a good toy."

And she was. My perfect, ruined toy.

Chapter Thirteen

Vivian

I shouldn't have liked it.

That was the first thought that flickered through my mind as I lay looking up at the beveled ceiling in the kitchen, trying to ignore the way my body had just betrayed me.

I had come.

Hard.

While spread out on Jeff's kitchen island with a glass water bottle inside me. I'd been so wet and desperate I was sure I'd thrust my hips while he'd fucked me with it.

I told myself I hadn't had a choice. It's what I'd agreed to when I'd sold myself the night before.

But even as I clung to that defense, heat curled low in my belly at the memory. The filthy things he'd said while I moaned and clenched around something that shouldn't have made me feel good.

What the hell was wrong with me?

I'd just been fucked with a bottle, *and I came*. I'd wanted it. Or maybe just my body had, which might have been worse because it meant I couldn't even trust myself.

My fingers traced the leather against my skin. The collar he'd buckled around my neck was still there. He still owned me.

And I was still wet.

I clearly had issues.

I should gather what dignity I had left and march out the door.

But that'd mean I'd lose out on sixty thousand dollars.

Yeah, that's it. I was staying for the money.

Not because I'd liked how he'd treated me or used me. It was for the money.

****

Jeff

By late afternoon, I'd stopped pretending I wasn't watching the clock.

She hadn't made a sound since I left her in the guest room. Maybe she was waiting for me to come get her.

I could do that.

Taking the stairs two at a time, I paused outside her door to catch my breath before I walked in.

She was under the covers with the comforter pulled tight around her when I opened the door.

"Time to wake up, whore. It's playtime."

She stirred beneath the comforter, blinking as she turned toward me. No words—just obedience.

"Out of bed. On all fours."

She remained still for half a breath, then moved. The blanket fell away, revealing her naked body, and fuck, that collar still looked perfect on her.

I leisurely circled the bed. "You've taken cock in your mouth and pussy. Now it's time to train your ass."

She tensed but didn't protest.

"Face down, ass up."

When she obeyed, I went to the drawer where I'd stashed the plug earlier—a gleaming steel one, small but weighty with a red jewel heart-shaped base. I bought the training set last night when I purchased her collar.

It was perfect for a start. I grabbed a bottle of lube and stepped behind her.

"You belong to me this month. That means every hole is mine."

I flipped the cap of the lube open, slicked the plug, then spread her cheeks apart with one hand and dribbled more lube on her pink star.

"This will stay in until I say otherwise," I said as I placed the tip to her tight hole. "And you'll thank me for making you useful."

She whimpered but didn't pull away.

"Good slut," I murmured as I pressed the metal in inch by inch. Although she trembled, she still held position. When it was seated fully, I gave it a tap. She gasped, then shocked the shit out of me when she murmured, "Thank you for making me useful, Sir."

Goddammit.

She wasn't *really* supposed to thank me. Not until I made her.

"On your feet."

She stood, legs slightly shaky. I told myself I didn't care.

"Follow me."

I led her to the den on the first floor, where the logs in the fireplace crackled softly and my laptop waited on my desk. I pointed to the cushion I'd placed on the floor beside my chair.

"Kneel."

She immediately sank to her knees.

"Hands on your thighs. Eyes down."

Again, she did what she was told without complaint.

I sat in my brown leather desk chair and opened my laptop.

"If that plug comes out, you'll regret it."

Then I got to work, catching up on reports while she knelt naked at my feet like I owned her.

Because I did.

For twenty-six more days, anyway.

****

Vivian

After an hour of kneeling at Jeff's feet, my back started to ache, and my thighs began to burn. But my pride refused to show him I was struggling.

Finally, he took my chin in his hand and tilted my head up so I was looking at him. His smile bordered on tender, which for me, was scary. Any time my father had been kind to me, it had always been a precursor to terror raining down.

"You're doing such a good job. Do you want to change positions?"

"Yes, Sir. Thank you."

I half-expected him to laugh and tell me, "Too bad," but he didn't.

"Lay on your stomach. I want to see the plug in your ass."

With relief, I turned away from him and dropped down onto the pillow, so my butt was on display. I didn't even care what I must have looked like with the red heart sparkling out of my behind.

I'm not sure how long I lay there. The warmth of the fire and the events of the last twenty-four hours caught up with me, and I fell into a light sleep.

The sound of his laptop clicking closed, followed by his chair rolling away from his desk pulled me awake, and I felt him kneel beside me to murmur in my ear, "Get on your hands and knees."

His command was direct, but his tone wasn't as cruel as it had been last night, or even this morning.

I did as he instructed and wasn't sure what to expect when I heard his zipper go down, and the cap of the lube bottle flip open.

He pulled the plug in my butt out an inch, then resituated it inside at the same time he shoved his cock deep in my pussy. With how easily he filled me, I realized he must have slicked his shaft.

Between his dick and the plug, I'd never felt fuller, or as good, and I bit back a moan.

"Fuck, I thought you were tight before," he growled as he pumped in and out of me. "You're even tighter now."

He pushed my face into the pillow while he drilled me without mercy.

He snarled, "Dirty slut with your fucking tight cunt making my cock so hard…" like it was a bad thing. "I'm going to come so deep inside you, you'll be dripping all damn week."

That visual was hot, and I felt myself edging closer to an orgasm, so I clenched my body to fight it. I knew he would not be happy if I came without permission.

He must have been able to tell I was close because I felt a sharp sting to my ass as he barked, "You better not come, whore!"

His fingers bit into my hips and his rhythm became erratic until finally he seated himself fully inside my pussy and let out a long grunt. "Fuck yesssss! Take it!"

I whimpered with need as I lay with my face on the pillow, ass still high in the air.

"You did a good job tonight," he murmured as he twisted the plug in my ass while his cock plugged his come in my pussy. "You didn't whine. Didn't squirm," he rotated the anal plug again. "Kept this in here like you were told to."

A flush crept down my neck. I hated the way his approval made me warm.

He pulled his cock and the plug out at the same time. I suddenly felt empty while his cum gushed down my inner thigh.

Using his finger and thumb, I felt him spread my pussy apart.

"Yeah, that's fucking hot," he mumbled as he smeared his cum around my folds. "I think you deserve a reward, whore."

He pushed his thumb inside my pussy and ordered, "Ride my hand, bitch."

I ground down on his thumb while he played my clit with his other hand like he knew every nerve by name.

Once again, I found myself teetering on the orgasmic cliff, and he growled, "Don't you dare fucking come until I tell you to."

The torture was so delicious, I wanted to scream. I opted for begging instead.

My movements faltered, and I cried, "Please, Master, may I come?"

He chuckled as he rubbed my clit faster.

"No."

Oh god. I wasn't sure I'd be able to hold out much longer.

Every muscle in my body went taut, and I was hanging on by a thread. A tear leaked from the corner of my eye, and my plea came out in a sob, "Please, Sir."

He whispered, "Come, whore," and the climax immediately overtook me. I shook from head to toe as pleasure shot through every cell of my being. I'd never experienced anything so incredible—it was almost too much. Just the thought of never feeling like that again was painful.

My body went limp, and I collapsed in a heap on the pillow.

Then I started to cry.

~~~~

I felt myself being lifted off the ground, then I was situated on his lap on the couch in his den.

His hand stroked my hair, and his deep voice was soothing when he softly said, "Don't cry, baby. You're safe. I've got you."

Wait... what?

I decided if I was dreaming, I didn't want to wake up and cried myself to sleep in his arms.

****

Jeff

I think I broke my new toy.

Chapter Fourteen

Vivian

I took a big stretch when I woke in the morning, then stopped halfway through.

Where the hell am I?

The scent hit me first: something clean and masculine, tinged with soap and sandalwood. *Jeff.* Or, as he liked to be referred to as, *Sir.*

I looked around the room; it was exactly how I envisioned his bedroom would look: all clean lines and muted tones. The slate-grey walls matched the fluffy comforter and window coverings, giving the space a nice cool, masculine feel, while the dark wood furniture added warmth. Floor-to-ceiling windows lined one wall, the kind that probably let in a flood of morning light if the electronic shades weren't lowered like they were now. It was minimalist, but not cold. Everything looked expensive and perfectly arranged. Like him.

Okay, so I figured out where I was, but the bigger question of *why* I was there had yet to be resolved.

His side of the mattress was empty, but the sheets were still warm. I was naked, except for the collar around my neck.

The events of last night came back to me. I remembered how he'd held me in his arms, whispering sweet words while running his hand up and down my back to comfort me.

I think he'd even called me "baby".

And now I woke up in his bed—without his cock gagging me.

I got out of bed and went to use the bathroom in the guest room I'd been using, After brushing my teeth and hair, and washing my face, I pulled the white t-shirt of his that I'd been wearing over my head and made my way down the stairs. My bare feet moved across the cool hardwood as I followed the smell of coffee. I wasn't sure what I expected, but the sight of him shirtless at the kitchen island, tablet in one hand and a spatula in the other, caught me off guard.

He looked relaxed, almost domestic. A far cry from the man who'd made me squirt in front of a roomful of men just thirty-six hours earlier.

He didn't look up right away. Just said, "Good morning, baby. Shower, then come eat. Don't take too long—I'm making breakfast."

Baby?

"Oh, okay." I quickly added, "Sir," because I still wasn't sure what was happening.

I turned without another word and headed back to the bathroom to start the shower.

As I waited for the water to warm up, I took off the t-shirt and unclasped the collar, carefully setting it on the vanity, far from the sink so there wouldn't be any accidents.

The hot water soothed my aching muscles and washed away the dried cum and lube, but it did nothing to help with the confusion swirling in my head.

Last night, he'd held me. Whispered to me. He'd called me baby and let me sleep in his bed.

I remembered feeling safe in his arms

Could someone so cold also be capable of tenderness?

I stepped out and dried off quickly then ran a brush through my wet hair.

The black leather collar sitting in stark contrast to the white marble reminded me that, no, this wasn't romance. This was transactional. I'd sold myself to him. So, whether he chose to be kind or cruel, it didn't matter. I was still just his property for the month.

But something in me wanted to believe this could be more. Maybe he was seeing me as something more than the whore he'd bought.

But then I went downstairs, and that thought evaporated into thin air.

~~~~

I walked back into the kitchen, still damp from the shower with Jeff's collar once again secured around my neck.

He didn't look at me. Just said, "Island. Up. Spread your legs."

I hesitated for a second, then climbed onto the counter without a word. The marble felt cool against my skin as I spread my legs like he wanted.

He turned toward the stove again and flipped something in the pan, like this was normal. Like my pussy on display was as routine as making eggs.

He didn't touch me at first. Just looked.

Then, casually, he reached over and ran two fingers between my folds before smirking. "You're wet, whore."

I didn't answer. I didn't know if it was from the shower or from being objectified. I guess to him, it didn't matter.

Another minute passed with my legs spread wide. He plated breakfast like nothing was out of place. Then his fingers brushed my clit, and he smirked again when I flinched.

My face burned. Not from embarrassment at having my pussy on display, but from how wet I knew I was becoming. Again. Just from being looked at and touched like a thing.

I hated how easy I made it for him.

But I didn't move. I stayed spread open, like his obedient whore on the counter, because that's what I was. That's what I'd agreed to be for the low, low price of one hundred thousand dollars.

Maybe the worst part wasn't being owned and used for his pleasure. It was how much I liked it.

****

Jeff

I let her eat at the table with me.

She looked unsure when I pulled out the chair, like it might be a trick. It wasn't. I just wanted to see her across from me, naked but for the collar. Mine.

I cut into my omelet and said, "What are you majoring in?"

She paused mid-bite to answer, "Psychology."

"Hmm." I wasn't sure why I thought it'd be something like business or education.

After taking a swig of coffee, I asked, "Favorite subject?"

"Social deviance." She smiled faintly, then pressed her lips together to quell it.

Of course it was.

I nodded. "That explains some things."

She didn't respond, just watched me for a moment. "Did you always want to be a doctor?"

"No, I have a trust fund, so I never thought much about what I wanted to be when I grew up while I was younger." I took a bite of my breakfast. "But by my second year in college, I realized I wanted to actually do something with my life. Do something that mattered. Medicine seemed to check all the boxes."

She nodded. "Do you like it?"

"I like having a purpose. And I like being in control."

She snorted, then her hand flew to her mouth to try to cover it up.

I couldn't help but smile. I mean, she wasn't wrong to laugh at that.

I decided to let it slide and continued. "And the pay is decent. I was able to buy this house without dipping into my trust."

"It's a beautiful home," she said softly.

I looked around the kitchen and tried to see it through her eyes. "I'm comfortable here. Plus, the block is quiet, and my neighbors aren't too nosy."

She looked down at her plate and pushed the omelet around with her fork. It was obvious she was trying to think of something to add. Finally, she asked, "What's your favorite food?"

I smiled. "Whatever you eat off my cock."

Her face turned up, her lips curled in a grin as she shook her head subtly at me, like I was her boyfriend whose jokes she was tolerating.

I liked that idea more than I should have.

We finished in silence after that. But it wasn't tense. Just... comfortable.

And that was the problem.

This was starting to feel normal.

And normal was dangerous. It made it too easy to forget she wasn't mine because she wanted to be. It was because I bought her. Just like every woman before her.

Chapter Fifteen

Jeff

"Do you like baseball?"

Vivian blinked at me like she wasn't sure it was a real question. I tilted my head toward the living room. "The Padres are on. Postseason."

She nodded. "I—I've never really watched."

"Not even when you were little?"

"No."

That surprised me. Most people grew up with at least a game on in the background on a Sunday afternoon. What the hell kind of dad didn't introduce his kid to baseball?

That's when it dawned on me. Maybe she never had a dad. That might also explain some things.

I stood and walked to the living room, flipping on the TV as I sat on the couch. She followed behind and stepped toward the sofa like she was going to sit next to me.

"What are you doing?"

She froze.

I tsked and shook my head as I pointed to the floor.

"Whores belong on the floor." I handed her a pillow similar to the one she'd knelt on last night. "On this. And bend over."

Her eyes flicked up to mine, like maybe she was expecting me to say, "Just kidding."

I wasn't.

I kept my expression stern, and she moved to the pillow, then leaned forward, hands flat on the floor, ass in the air to present herself like the obedient little thing she was turning out to be.

"Good whore," I murmured as I reached for the bigger plug I'd set aside for today. "Gonna stretch you a bit more," I said as I lubed the metal. "You're not ready for my cock back here yet, but you will be."

The plug slid in with a slow push, and her breath hitched. I gave it a small twist, then tapped it to make sure it was in.

"Keep it in. If it falls out, I'll make you lick it clean."

She didn't say a word. Just got back into position on the floor like nothing had happened.

I stared at the screen, pretending to focus on the game, but my cock was already getting hard, and not because of the score.

Because of the fact that I could do anything I wanted to her.

Because I owned her.

She stayed on the pillow at my feet, naked, quiet, and still while I watched the game.

I absentmindedly reached down to stroke her hair like she was a good pet, and she closed her eyes at my touch.

Like she liked it.

Like she liked *me*. But I knew that wasn't possible.

She couldn't. I wouldn't let her.

This wasn't about affection, it was about ownership. Nothing else.

So, when my cock stirred again half an inning later, I told myself it wasn't from lust. It was power.

Power to take her whenever I wanted.

I set the remote down and snapped my fingers. "Up."

She stood without question.

"Over the arm of the couch. Now."

She bent over, and I pulled the plug from her, then tossed it on the cushion beside us before reaching for the lube. After giving myself a quick stroke, I lined up and shoved in where the plug had stretched her, slow but relentless, until I bottomed out in her ass.

"Fuck. So tight," I growled as I sank in deeper. "Taking it like you were made for this."

She whimpered into the couch, and I reached around to find her clit, already slick and swollen. Just a few circles, and she moaned, "So good."

I grinned against her shoulder but kept my voice stern. "You better not come, whore."

Her body quivered beneath me. I could feel how close she was.

I leaned over her back, my voice a low threat against her ear as I repeated myself. "Don't you dare fucking come."

A muffled moan escaped her throat, and her fingers clutched the cushion, but she obeyed.

Gripping her hips, I fucked her hard, rough, and deep. No rhythm. No tenderness. Just pure, brutal possession.

She didn't cry or beg. Just took it like she was supposed to.

I drove into her one final time and held her tight against my hips as I buried my cock deep and emptied my balls inside her ass.

When I pulled out, I grabbed the plug and shoved it back in place, sealing my cum inside her.

"Stay like that."

She nodded once, hair tangled, lips parted.

I took my seat and grabbed the remote, flipping the game back on.

"You can sit back down," I said without looking at her.

She didn't move right away, and I could tell she wanted to challenge me. But after a beat, she thought better of it and settled on the pillow at my feet.

Smart girl.

And that's how I watched the rest of the inning—with her plugged, used, and silent on the floor, while I'd bet my paycheck she was dripping with need.

Too bad.

I came; it didn't matter that she hadn't.

****

Vivian

By the time he finally looked at his watch and stood, my ass was half-numb from sitting in a position that kept the plug in. But my pussy was still throbbing.

"It's four forty-five. Go get your things; the club's car will be here at five to take you home."

I struggled to get up, and he reached down to offer me a hand. Once I was upright, he pressed on my shoulders to bend me over the couch. Without a word, he removed the red gem from my ass. The minute it was free, his cum spilled down my thighs.

He didn't seem to care and just nodded toward the doorway leading to the stairs, like I was dismissed.

I didn't speak. Didn't react. Simply turned and headed to get my things while his semen ran down my legs as if it was an everyday occurrence.

I shut the guest room door behind me and leaned against it. I was horny and pissed that I couldn't do anything about it. And his cum leaking down my thighs had turned cold and sticky, which seemed appropriate.

In the bathroom, I grabbed a washcloth and ran it under hot water, then cleaned myself up as best I could before toweling dry.

The collar stayed on. Of course it did. He'd told me I wasn't to take it off until our contract ended.

Back in the bedroom, I opened my overnight bag and pulled out the olive-green dress I'd packed.

It was tight, showed an ample amount of cleavage, had long sleeves, and the hem hit just above the knee.

I slipped into it and grabbed clean underwear, but even as I pulled the silky panties on, I knew I was breaking one of his rules.

Too fucking bad.

I guess he should have taken care of my needs if he wanted my pussy exposed and available so badly.

Fucking asshole.

I didn't care what his rules were; I was using my vibrator when I got home.

He could suck it.

~~~~

I made my way downstairs, trying to ignore the ache between my legs and the slickness I could still feel even after cleaning up. I was dressed, packed, and going home to have a revenge date with my vibrator, because fuck him for leaving me this way.

At least, that was the plan.

Jeff was waiting in the entry, leaning one shoulder against the stair railing. His gaze dropped, and I could tell the moment he spotted the panty line beneath my dress.

"You're wearing underwear," he said flatly.

I didn't answer. It wasn't like I could deny it.

He stepped forward, and in two strides, he was on me. His fingers hooked the waistband beneath my dress and yanked—hard. The panties tore and dropped to the floor.

"Your holes stay available to me. Always. Don't make me tell you that again."

I was pissed enough that my mouth started working before my brain caught up.

I raised my chin and defiantly asked, "Or what?"

He shook his head and muttered, "Oh, little girl..." Then without another word, he shoved my back against the door. His hand closed around my throat—not hard, just firm enough to remind me who was in control.

My breath caught as he hiked up the hem of my dress.

"You think you're going to walk out of here like you're in charge?"

His fingers slid between my thighs and found me soaked. He didn't smile or gloat. Just shoved two fingers inside me while his thumb pressed down on my clit.

I gasped, clinging to his forearm as my knees buckled. I was so close it was pathetic.

"Take it," he snarled. "Come now, or not at all."

It only took a few rough strokes, and my body shattered against his hand. I cried out, holding on to him in order to stay upright.

He held me there a moment, then withdrew his fingers and wiped them down my thigh, slow and deliberate.

"Don't ever sass me again. Do you understand? Or I'll deny you another orgasm for the rest of our time together."

The only thing I could do was murmur, "Yes, Sir," while he picked up my bag and opened the door.

****

Jeff

I grabbed her overnight bag and walked outside, not bothering to wait to see if she followed me.

The town car waited in the circular drive with the driver standing beside it in a dark suit and cap. It was a different one than we'd had on Friday. He opened the back door when he saw us walk down the steps.

Vivian didn't say anything, just walked with her chin high and her mouth tight.

Her defiant energy radiated off her, and I didn't bother to try and understand why that turned me on so fucking much.

She breezed past me without so much as a, "See you next weekend," and slid into the backseat, smoothing her skirt and shifting to sit primly.

Oh, I don't think so.

I leaned into the back seat and grabbed her knees, opening them wide.

"Not like that. Keep your legs spread the whole ride."

Her nostrils flared, but she didn't speak. Just kept her thighs wide.

I reached under the hem of her dress and dragged it up to her waist, baring her freshly fingered cunt. "You leave it like this. Don't you dare close your legs."

Her jaw clenched, but she didn't respond, although if looks could kill...

"And don't forget—you're expected to wear your collar even when you're not here. And you better not touch yourself. At all. You come when I say, not before."

She gave the smallest nod but looked straight ahead, refusing to spare a glance in my direction.

I stood and met the driver's eyes.

"She's mine. You can look, but you better not touch. Don't even fucking speak to her."

The man gave a tight nod and got in the driver's seat, and I shut the door and stepped back.

I watched the taillights disappear down my drive and told myself it was good she was gone.

I didn't need her here, distracting me when I was supposed to be working.

Nor did I need her sassy mouth, or the way she looked at me like I was something more than the man who bought her.

She was just a whore I paid to use for a month. That's all.

She didn't mean anything to me.

At least, that's what I kept telling myself.

Chapter Sixteen

Vivian

My phone buzzed just after ten on Monday morning. I was wide awake but still in bed, curled on my side and clutching a pillow as I replayed the weekend's events over in my head for the hundredth time. I smiled when I saw Kit's name flash across the screen, surprised she'd waited until midmorning to call.

"Hey hot stuff."

My BFF didn't waste time. "How did it go? Tell me everything!"

I rolled onto my back and stared at the peeling paint on my ceiling. "It was... intense. Right from the start."

She exhaled into the line. "Yeah, I heard what happened after the auction. The table and the crowd."

Of course she had. The sex club might be exclusive, but gossip traveled fast, especially when someone got publicly humiliated and made to come in front of an audience.

If there was anyone I could be honest with, it was Kit.

"He made me squirt in front of a room full of people, and they all cheered. Then he made me come, and they cheered *again*. But instead of being horrified, I was turned on. In fact, I can't stop thinking about it." My throat tightened. "What the fuck is wrong with me?"

She didn't hesitate when she replied, "Absolutely nothing. You're allowed to like what you like."

"I mean, it was humiliating. I should've hated it—"

"Did you consider using your safe word?"

I blinked at the ceiling. "I, uh, never told him what it was."

"What?" Kit snapped. "Viv, what the hell?"

"I know," I said quickly. "But the truth is... I don't think I would've used it. Not once this whole weekend." I pressed the phone to my ear and exhaled. "Even though it was a lot."

"Like good-a lot, or you're curled in a ball questioning your life choices-a lot?"

"Both?" I winced. "It wasn't what I expected. He was... rough and controlling. But also... not."

"Not?"

"He held me after. Told me I was safe." I paused. "Then the next morning, he made me eat breakfast after he'd had me lie with my legs spread on the counter while he cooked."

"Holy shit."

"Yeah. It was degrading. And I was so wet I wanted to die."

Kit let out a low whistle. "Girl..."

"I know, I'm fucked up." I covered my face with a pillow as I listened to her response.

She didn't miss a beat "No, you're not. But if it doesn't feel right, you need to use a safe word."

"It does," I whispered. "That's what scares me."

"Babe, you're two consenting adults, you do you. Let that freak flag fly."

"I didn't even know I had a freak flag until Friday."

"Well, now you do. Enjoy it, and don't feel ashamed about it."

I was still coming to grips with this new side of me. "I'll try my best."

"So, you're at your apartment until Friday? Does that mean you're working this week?"

I nodded even though she couldn't see me. "Yeah. I've got the night shift tonight and Thursday, and the lunch shift Tuesday and Wednesday. I really need the money."

There was a pause. "Do you feel okay going back?"

"It's just dancing," I said quickly. "I've done it a thousand times."

But even as the words left my mouth, something about them felt off. Like maybe it wasn't just dancing anymore. Had I always had a voyeur kink and just never knew it?

"Let me know if you want to hang out sometime this week."

"I will. Thanks for checking on me."

"Of course. You're my ride or die. I'm not going to let anything bad happen to you."

If only it were that simple.

My dad was dead, but the loan sharks he owed didn't care, and I'd sold myself to protect my mom, sister, and family dog.

Now I was collared, used, and fucked—in more ways than one.

And part of me wanted more.

I didn't have time to unpack it, a thousand dollar loan shark payment was due, and I was still a couple hundred short. I had a night shift to make.

By seven, I was back onstage at the club, strutting around with pasties on my nipples while the bass thumped through the speakers.

Same stage, same pole, but something was different now. It was me.

I used to feel powerful up here, like I was the one in control.

But tonight, as I wrapped myself around the pole and dropped into a slow grind, it didn't feel like power.

It felt hollow. Pure muscle memory without a trace of seduction.

I went through the motions. Made eye contact. Blew kisses.

But my body remembered something else.

Rough hands. A voice telling me to spread wider. The ache of being used and owned.

And I hated how much I missed that.

****

Jeff

It was Wednesday, and I hadn't been able to focus since Monday.

A patient file sat open in front of me, but I'd read the same line four times without processing a single word.

But it wasn't work that had me distracted, it was her.

Vivian.

This whole thing had started as a way to punish her for turning me down that night at the masquerade, then picking someone else.

Fucking Bradford.

So, I'd bought her.

I'd outbid the bastard just to bring her to her knees and remind her who she rejected.

It should've been satisfying, and for a while, it was.

But now?

I leaned back in my chair and dragged a hand down my face. I could still feel the weight of her on the pillow at my feet. Still hear that soft gasp when I'd shoved my cock in her ass. Still see the way she smiled, just a little, when she told me her favorite subject was social deviance.

She was supposed to be my whore. One month to control and use.

So why the fuck did I keep thinking about how she looked eating eggs across from me? Why did that little snort when I told her I liked control stick in my head?

That moment had been too real. Too... normal. She'd looked at me like I was something more than just her owner. And worse, I'd liked it.

I told myself this was about power and teaching her a lesson. She didn't really matter. At least not beyond the contract.

Still, I should've gotten her number.

Not to talk or check in to see how she was doing, but just to make sure she was following the rules.

That was all.

Chapter Seventeen

Vivian

I checked my appearance in the mirror one last time, then put on the biometrics bracelet the club mandated I wear when I spent the weekend with Jeff and waited by the window.

Finally, the familiar black town car pulled in front of my rundown apartment building. It looked so out of place there, and frankly, I didn't want my neighbors to know it was me getting picked up, lest they think my apartment had something worth robbing while I was gone for the weekend. So, I grabbed my purse and the bag I'd packed and hurried out the door.

The waiting driver was Tom, the one who'd driven us to Jeff's place on Friday after the auction. He smirked when he opened my door. "Going back for more, eh?"

"Seems that way," I said coolly as I slid in the backseat, leaving my bag outside for him to deal with.

For a second, I panicked and thought he was going to drive away and leave it sitting at the curb, but I heard the trunk open then close before he slid behind the wheel.

I noticed him watching me through the rearview mirror, so I took out my phone to have something to look at besides him. I really didn't want to have a conversation. My nerves were rattled and I wanted to try and settle down on the drive.

"You look beautiful, by the way."

I offered him a polite smile. "Thanks."

I hoped Jeff thought so, too. I'd taken great care getting ready, so he'd approve of my appearance. Of course, I'd cursed myself that I even gave a damn what he thought.

But I did.

I hadn't even packed panties this time and had even bought some crotchless black lingerie at Walmart that I thought he might like. I'd also picked up some cute dresses that were on sale.

Tom kept looking back, and I realized he was trying to look under my dress.

I really wanted to find that button that brought the divider up.

"How much do you make, anyway?"

I decided to play dumb when I looked back at him in the mirror.

"I'm not sure what you mean."

"You don't have to give me an exact number, just a ballpark. Maybe I could get a few of my friends together and we could come up with enough to buy you for a night. I bet you're a wild little thing."

Not in a million years, buddy.

I gave him a saccharine smile.

"Sixty thousand."

"Bullshit."

I cocked my head, and he continued. "You live in a dump. No way do you make sixty grand a trick."

I shrugged. "Wanna bet?"

He drove a little before he mumbled, "I hope he's getting his money's worth."

Oh, he is.

My heartrate picked up when the car turned into Jeff's neighborhood. Was I actually excited to see him?

I hated to admit it, but yeah, I was.

I didn't like how we'd left things on Sunday and hoped he didn't hold a grudge.

We started up the winding drive, and I willed myself to take a deep breath as I fidgeted with my collar.

The car rolled to a stop in Jeff's driveway, and Tom got out to grab my bag from the trunk. I reached for the door handle, but he was already there, opening the back door like he thought he was being chivalrous instead of doing his job.

As I stepped out, he leaned in and said, "Let me know your bottom-line price. I'll see how much I can scrape together."

I scoffed, then froze when I saw the front door fly open.

Jeff stood in the entryway, one hand braced on the frame, the other hanging loose at his side, except his fingers flexed like he was imagining them around someone's throat.

His voice cut across the drive, cold and lethal. "What the fuck did you just say to her?"

****

Jeff

I'd been watching the driveway feed, phone in hand, waiting to make sure the car arrived without issue. That was the excuse, anyway. Truth was, I wanted to see her the moment she stepped out.

And when she did, fuck me.

Her hair was down, legs bare beneath a short, black dress, and her collar fastened perfectly in place. She looked stunning. My cock twitched just looking at her.

Then the driver leaned in and said something.

I tapped the volume.

"...Let me know your bottom-line price. I'll see how much I can scrape together."

My vision went red, and I threw open the front door and stalked down the steps.

"What the fuck did you just say to her?"

Tom turned, startled. "Sir, I didn't—"

"Don't lie to me."

He took a step back. "It was a joke."

"You think I'm laughing?"

Vivian stood frozen beside the car, lips parted in shock. I didn't even look at her. All my fury was aimed at the asshole who thought he could talk to her like that.

His mouth opened like he was going to argue, but one look must've told him better. He climbed into the driver's seat, and I leaned down so only he could hear.

"If you ever speak to her like that again, I will break your fucking jaw and make sure you're blackballed from every private client in the state. Do you understand me?"

"Yes, sir."

"Drive. And don't come back."

Tom pulled away slowly, eyes on the rearview mirror the whole time. I didn't move until the car turned the corner and disappeared from sight.

Then I turned to her.

She didn't speak. Just stared like she wasn't sure what to say.

Hell, I wasn't either.

She looked too good, dammit. That tight dress, that collar. I was happy to see her, and that pissed me off. I hated that I'd missed her. That some part of me had been counting down the days since she left.

This wasn't supposed to matter.

"Get in the house," I said, my jaw tight. "And for fuck's sake, take off that damn dress."

***

Vivian

That's it? No, *hello*. No, *you look nice*. Just an order to get inside and strip.

The dress I'd picked out—tight in the waist, flared at the hips, long enough to be elegant but short enough to tempt—suddenly felt ridiculous. I'd spent half the afternoon getting ready, curling my hair, redoing my makeup twice, standing in front of the mirror trying to guess what he'd want to see when I stepped out of the car.

Apparently, I'd guessed wrong.

"Nice to see you, too," I snarked as I stepped past him, my heels clicking as I walked up the steps. The house smelled familiar when I walked through the door this time, and somehow that made it worse.

I'd wondered all week if he was going to pick up where we left off last Sunday, or if we were going to start anew. Apparently, he'd chosen the "hold a grudge" option.

The door shut behind him, and I stood there awkwardly with my bag in my hand, unsure what to do next.

Did I strip right there in the entry? Take off the dress that he clearly hated? Or should I retreat to the guest room to change?

Fuck it.

I dropped the bag and reached behind me to tug the zipper down, then slipped out of the arms and shimmied to get the form fitting dress past my hips. I leaned down and retrieved it from my feet, then folded it over my arm, as if standing in his entryway in only heels, bra, and a collar was totally normal.

"I'm assuming I'll be in the same room as last time?"

He didn't say a word. Just took his sweet time to rake his gaze from my head to my toes and back again, his jaw tight the entire time. His eyes were unreadable except for the briefest flicker of something softer I couldn't name.

"Guest room's the same," he finally said, his voice flat. "Put your bag away, then come find me. My cock needs servicing, whore."

I didn't argue. I knew my place. And the filthy way he reminded me lit a spark in my belly. My pussy was already wet, aching to be used.

My therapist was going to earn her paycheck in our next session.

****

Jeff

I watched her walk away with her hips swaying and that luscious ass I wanted to bite. Or ruin. Probably both.

Fuck.

She turned me on, there was no point pretending otherwise. But I needed to get a handle on it—on *her*.

Because the second I saw her step out of that car, every rational thought flew straight to hell. And I couldn't afford that. Not with her.

She was supposed to be mine to control. Not the other way around.

I wasn't going to pretend I didn't want her, but I still planned to remind her what this was—what *she* was.

Not my girlfriend. Not my partner.

Just a warm hole with manners that I owned for three more weeks. Last Sunday, she'd needed a reminder of that.

She was damn lucky she hadn't been wearing panties when she stepped out of that dress just now. If she had, I would've ripped them off her and stuffed them in her mouth before I bent her over the stairs and fucked her ass without any lube.

She hadn't said a word of protest when I told her my cock needed servicing. In fact, I could have sworn her pupils dilated a little.

Ah, I think sweet Vivian liked her role as my whore.

I liked it, too.

But what had concerned me this week was how much I'd thought about *her*, not just her holes.

I needed to get that shit under control. I didn't get the happy ending unless I paid for it. And I was only paid up for three more weeks.

I'd barely settled at my desk in the den when she strutted in with no hesitation. Without a word, she walked across the room with her hips swaying as the ring of my collar jingled and caught the light.

I spun in my chair and unbuttoned my pants, then pulled my hard cock out. She sank to her knees between my legs and got to work without being told.

I leaned back in my chair as I fisted her hair and pushed her head down until she gagged.

"That's it whore. Choke on that dick."

Fuck.

It was good to be me.

Chapter Eighteen

Vivian

I woke to the smell of coffee wafting into my room. That meant he was up and in the kitchen. I quickly made myself presentable and headed downstairs.

He stood at the stove in pajama pants slung low on his hips, and nothing else.

Damn, he was hot.

With a spatula in one hand, and a coffee mug in the other, his expression was unreadable as he flipped something in the skillet.

He didn't look up when I entered. In fact, he didn't acknowledge me at all.

Fine. I could play my part.

I crossed the kitchen, climbed onto the island, and spread my legs wide, resting back on my hands so my used pussy was on display for him. I didn't say anything either, just waited.

His pause was subtle, a slight hitch in the movement of his arm, but I noticed it.

Still, he didn't look at me.

His voice was low when he finally said, "You're learning." He slid the pan's contents onto a plate. "Good girl."

My toes curled at the praise.

God, I was broken.

****

Jeff

I took one look at her pink, glistening pussy on display and decided that breakfast could wait.

Setting the plate on the counter by the stove, I shoved my pants down just enough to free my cock, lined up, and slammed inside her in one brutal thrust. She gasped and arched her back while I used her body like it was mine—because it was. For two weeks and six days more, every hole of hers belonged to me, and I intended to get my money's worth.

I didn't pace myself.

I wanted her sloppy with my cum leaking out of her during breakfast.

Thrust after thrust, I pounded into her. My fingers gripped her hips as I fucked her hard. Her bouncing tits added to my visual stimulation.

I didn't let her come, but I did with a long groan as I buried my face in her neck and seated myself deep inside her cunt.

After my breathing evened out, I stepped away and tucked myself back in my pants like she was just a toy I'd finished using and set aside.

"Don't wipe," I ordered as I went back to the stove. I wanted her sloppy and dripping during breakfast. "Sit down at the table."

She slid off the island and winced as she sat, my cum already dripping onto the chair.

Perfect.

I put the plates in the microwave for thirty seconds and while I waited, refilled my coffee and served her a cup.

After setting her mug in front of her, I reached down to spread her pussy apart and admire my handiwork.

"Beautiful," I murmured then with a spring in my step, retrieved the plates from the microwave.

She raised her coffee to her lips trying to hide her smile, but I saw it in her eyes. They were warm and playful. And too damn comfortable.

"What?" I asked, arching a brow.

"You're being almost nice. Should I be worried?"

I leaned back in my chair. "Don't confuse civility with softness. I just came. Give me a few minutes."

She laughed softly and cut her omelet with her fork. "So... how old are you?"

I blinked at the change in topic. "Why?"

"Just curious. You know how old I am. Seems fair."

"Thirty-six."

She paused, her fork halfway to her mouth. "Damn. You wear it well."

I cocked my head. "Is that supposed to be a compliment?"

"It is. Just don't start calling me 'kiddo' or anything. That'd ruin the whole vibe."

I let out a quiet laugh. "Noted. As long as you don't call me 'daddy'."

Her button nose wrinkled, and she replied, "Ew, never. You don't have to worry about that."

I knew there was a story there but didn't push it.

For a moment, it was quiet. Just two people having breakfast. Except one of us was dripping cum.

"You're leaking on my chair," I noted.

She responded with a smirk. "Whose fault is that?"

"Mine," I said, meeting her eyes. "That's exactly what you're supposed to do."

She swallowed, and I could tell something was on her mind by the way she wouldn't look at me while she ate.

Finally, after a beat, she asked, "Do you ever bring anyone here... for real? Not as part of a contract?"

I didn't answer right away.

Then I said, "No. Never," and left it at that.

Chapter Nineteen

Vivian

I woke to the feel of soft sheets and the faint scent of his sandalwood cologne on the pillow beside mine. For a second, I didn't move, just lay there blinking at the ceiling while trying to figure out why I wasn't in the guest room.

Because last night, he'd told me to stay.

He'd taken what he wanted, still rough and controlling, but then he'd pulled me against his chest afterward and whispered, *Go to sleep, baby.*

Not *whore*.

Baby.

That shouldn't have meant anything; it was just a word; two syllables.

But it felt like it spoke volumes.

And that's what scared me.

Because while I liked being his whore, probably more than I cared to admit, I'd started liking the man who called me that too.

His kindness would only complicate things.

Because no matter how soft his grip felt wrapped around my waist, I couldn't forget what this was: a contract. A countdown.

Two more weekends. Then it was over.

He was a doctor, and I was a stripper who'd sold myself to him, and this wasn't *Pretty Woman*.

I'd be best served to remember that.

Steam filled the bathroom as I rinsed the conditioner from my hair. I hadn't heard the door open, and I jumped when I opened my eyes and saw him standing just outside the glass-block shower wall of the guest bath, dressed in a pair of jeans and a grey San Diego State hoodie.

"Oh my gosh, you scared me!"

"Sorry, I thought you heard me come in. You need to get ready when you're done in here. Put on something warm and wear comfortable shoes."

"I don't have anything warm. I only brought dresses; that's all I'm allowed—remember?"

"Fine, we'll stop by your apartment so you can change."

My stomach dipped and I thought about how Tom had described my apartment building as a dump. I didn't want Jeff to see how I lived.

He must have noticed my hesitation because he asked, "What? I'm not going to stalk you if that's what you're worried about."

I turned the water off and wrung out my hair.

"I'm not worried about that." He handed me a towel, and I rubbed it over my legs. "Where are we going?"

"A festival."

That was it. No smile or explanation.

"Like a fall festival? With apple cider and pumpkins?"

"I guess. I thought you'd appreciate having something to do other than choke on my dick."

"How chivalrous of you."

"I know, right? So, get ready, and we'll swing by your apartment so you can put on a pair of leggings and a sweatshirt."

He turned to leave, then stopped.

"But, Vivian?"

Vivian! He called me by my name!

I tried to sound nonchalant when I said, "Yeah?"

"Still no panties."

I fought not to roll my eyes when I quipped, "Wouldn't dream of it, Sir."

"See, that's the problem. You have, and you did."

"And then you taught me a lesson."

He chuckled darkly. "That I did." He glanced at his watch and announced, "You've got eighteen minutes."

"You know," I called after him, "it's a good thing we have a contract, because if you were really my boyfriend, I'd tell you to kick rocks with your timer bullshit."

His smile was menacing when he poked his head back around the corner and replied, "But we do have a contract. And if you want to get paid like the whore that you are, you'll be ready in"—he looked at his watch again—"seventeen minutes."

There it was. *Whore*. Not *baby*, not *Vivian*. I was back to being *whore*.

That was probably for the best. It made things less confusing that way.

"I'll be ready, *Master*."

****

Jeff

We turned off the main drag and the neighborhood got sketchier the farther we drove—cracked sidewalks, boarded-up businesses, bars on the windows, and graffiti everywhere you looked. Vivian shifted in her seat and pointed left.

"Turn here."

We wound through a cluster of rundown apartment complexes that needed more than just new stucco and fresh paint. The whole block should've been bulldozed and rebuilt from the foundation up.

She nodded at a rundown building in the middle of equally rundown ones.

"This is me," she said quietly.

I pulled in, my jaw tightening as I parked. My Porsche didn't belong here. *She* didn't belong here.

"I'll be quick," she said, already reaching for the handle. "You can park in the lot over there"—she gestured to a lot full of weeds and potholes, surrounded by a chain-link fence that sagged in places—"or just wait here."

"I'll just wait here." Partly because I didn't want to leave my car unattended, and partly because if I followed her up those stairs, I might ask what the fuck she was doing living in a place like this.

She disappeared inside the building, and I locked the doors. My fingers tapped restlessly against the steering wheel as I scanned the lot. A pair of tennis shoes tied together hung from a telephone wire, and graffiti covered a boarded-up unit two doors down while a guy slept on a bench beside a shopping cart on the other side of the chain-link fence.

Jesus.

She came back five minutes later in black leggings, an oversized pink sweatshirt, and a pair of white tennis shoes.

"All set," she said flashing a smile that was too bright to be real as she climbed in and buckled her seatbelt.

I knew she was embarrassed. Hell, *I* was embarrassed for her.

"You planning to use the money from this arrangement to move?"

She hesitated. "I wish it were that simple."

I glanced over. "Meaning?"

Vivian blew out a breath. "My dad died a few months ago. He drank himself to death and left my mom with a lot of debt. Like, *a lot* of debt. The loan-shark kind. I did the auction to pay Lorenzo so he wouldn't cut my mom's fingers off."

What the fuck?

I knew there had to be something up with her dad.

"And your cut from the club is going to cover it?"

"It's a start. I'm hoping it buys us some time, anyway."

I didn't say anything. Just drove.

But I couldn't get the image of her in that apartment building out of my head. She didn't belong there, of that I was certain.

An image of her in my bed when I woke up this morning popped into my head, like *that* was where she belonged.

I gave myself an internal shake.

No, she doesn't belong there either.

But I wasn't as convinced about that.

~~~~

The church lot was already full by the time we pulled in, so I parked in a gravel overflow near the back fence. We walked toward the entrance in silence, but I absentmindedly reached over and took her hand as we passed hay bales, orange lights, and pumpkins. The faint sound of a fiddle from a small stage near the food trucks filled the air, along with the smell of cinnamon and the crunch of fall leaves beneath our feet.

A kid ran past us with his face painted like a jack-o'-lantern, dragging a balloon by a string. Another tripped over a cornstalk and started wailing.

Vivian slowed when we passed a table stacked with little jars of honey and homemade jam.

"You ever come to one of these growing up?" I asked.

She shook her head. "No. We didn't do stuff like this."

I didn't press, although from what she'd told me, I wasn't surprised.

As if trying to defend herself, she continued, "I mean, San Diego doesn't exactly have a fall, you know?"

"That's true."

I motioned toward the tables lined with crafts. "If you see anything you want, let me know."

Her smile was almost childlike when she replied, "I will."

We walked around like a regular couple in the crowd. I should have been alarmed at how normal it felt to hold her hand and smile back at her whenever she got excited over a new find on one of the card tables filled with what she called treasures.

I thought it was all crap, but I kept that to myself. I was an asshole, but I wasn't going to rain on her parade. Especially since I was the one who'd brought us here in the first place.

****

Vivian

"This is so fun," I said as I leaned my head against his shoulder while we waited in line for warm apple cider. "Thank you for bringing me here."

He winked at me. "You can thank me on the way home."

I gave his jeans pocket a subtle squeeze as I murmured, "I'd be happy to."

He leaned down and whispered in my ear, "Be careful, baby, or you might just find yourself bent over a hay bale in a corner somewhere with my cock in your ass." Then he added, "But you'd probably like that."

He wasn't wrong, but it didn't feel like a compliment. More like a reminder of what I really was. His whore.

I appreciated that because in the moment it had been easy to pretend I was something more, like his girlfriend.

I simply smiled and agreed. "You're probably right, Sir."

Just then a group of boys in face paint, probably around ten years old, sprinted past us and tried to climb the hay bales. One got his feet tangled and tumbled backward, landing in a weird position so the bottom part of his leg looked like it was bent in the wrong direction. It made me wince, and the kid screamed bloody murder.

Jeff told me, "I'll be right back," and headed to where the kid's parents were now kneeling next to the hurt boy.

I saw Jeff talk to the couple, then he crouched down and said something to the little boy, who was still crying in pain, but the cries became quieter when Jeff placed his hand over the boy's much smaller one.

Jeff then went about directing people from the crowd that had gathered. He hadn't lied when he'd told me he liked to be in control, even at work.

He needed scissors. Someone from one of the booths produced a pair, and while continuing to speak quietly to the boy, he carefully cut the leg of the child's jeans away in order for him to get a better look.

I could tell it wasn't good by the grimace on his face.

Fortunately, someone must have called 911, because a young guy and girl dressed in EMT uniforms appeared with a gurney. Jeff directed them on what pain meds to administer and how to transfer the kid onto the board. Jeff hadn't released the boy's hand until he was safely strapped to the gurney. Then he touched the kid's shoulder and told him he was going to be okay, and that he was one brave kid.

The little boy nodded, a shaky smile on his tear-stained face while he tried to be as brave as Jeff was making him out to be.

That was the moment I knew I was in trouble because I might have fallen in love with Dr. Jeff Connolly right then.

Jeff handed the boy's father what looked like his card, and I heard him tell the man, "I mostly work at the VA, so I couldn't take him as a patient, but if you run into any trouble at the hospital, or need a second opinion, give me a call. I'll be happy to help."

The parents were so grateful and shook his hand vigorously before escorting their son to the waiting ambulance.

I just stared at Jeff when he returned to my side.

"What?" he asked with a grin.

"Can we go now? I really need you to fuck me."

Chapter Twenty

Vivian

I worked a double Monday and another on Tuesday. By the end of my afternoon shift on Wednesday, I could barely feel my legs, but I worked the night shift anyway.

It wasn't about the money; it was about being too busy to think. If I stayed moving, there was no room to even consider I might have fucked up and fallen in love with the man who'd bought me at an auction. No room to remember how he'd helped that little boy at the festival like some kind of hero, or how afterward, he'd bent me over the trunk of his Porsche like a villain and fucked me until I came so hard, I forgot my own name.

So, I worked, shaking my tits and ass onstage, then grinding on strangers' laps until their twenty dollars' worth of time was up, I felt wetness in their pants, or they handed me another twenty bucks.

Backstage, a girl named Fallon asked why I was working so much this week. I told her rent was due. It wasn't a lie, just not the whole truth.

Yeah, the money was great, but if my phone was in my locker, I couldn't check it to see if he'd texted. Or be disappointed that he hadn't. I was silly enough to think maybe he would, that's why he'd insisted we exchange numbers.

Then Thursday afternoon, as I lay on my couch listening to a true crime podcast on my tablet, my phone dinged. I practically tripped over the coffee table as I lunged for it.

Jeff: You better be wearing your collar.

Six freaking words, and I was as giddy as a schoolgirl.

Me: Of course, Sir.
Jeff: Good whore.

My stupid toes curled.

I never expected to miss someone who treated me like property.

But I did.

Friday morning, I gave myself a pep talk. I needed to get my head on straight.

He wasn't my boyfriend. He was *my temporary owner*.

On the ride to his house, I got wet thinking about how I hoped he proved just that when I arrived.

****

Jeff

I told myself I didn't care she hadn't texted. She didn't owe me that—I hadn't bought her time during the week.

Still, Thursday afternoon, I opened the app tied to the chip in her collar, just to check that she was wearing it.

The location signal blinked steady at her building. She hadn't taken it off.

Good girl.

I closed the app, then reopened it five minutes later. Just to be sure.

Pathetic.

The whole point of this arrangement was control over her. She gave me her body, her obedience, her holes, and in return, I gave her protection and a fucking payout.

Nothing more.

So why did I keep thinking about her mouth around my cock? Or the way she'd smiled at that damn Harvest Festival? Or how she'd looked curled up in my bed, wearing my collar like it meant something?

I should've had someone else picked by now. Another girl to keep me busy until Friday. Instead, I was watching her dot on a map like some obsessed freak with a GPS fetish.

I finally gave in and typed a message, even though I already knew the answer.

Me: You better be wearing your collar.

Three dots appeared.

Vivian: Of course, Sir.
Me: Good ~~girl~~.

I backspaced and tried again.

Me: Good whore.

I didn't send anything else. I didn't need to.

She was wearing her collar and answering my texts right away. She was still mine.

For now.

And it was starting to piss me off that I cared that it wasn't longer.

Chapter Twenty-One

Vivian

The car ride to his house was quiet this time. I had a new driver, Toby. Thank God. The man behind the wheel had greeted me with a curt nod as he opened the door for me, then took my bag, put it in the trunk, and got behind the wheel.

"511 Brookstone Drive?" he asked as he pulled away from the curb.

"Um... I'm not sure. Dr. Connolly's house."

He nodded and said, "That's the one," then was silent the rest of the drive.

My phone buzzed as we drove toward his neighborhood.

Jeff: I have an emergency at the hospital and won't be there when you arrive.

Jeff: The code for the front door is 0-5-1-1, then press the star button. Be waiting for me in the living room.

No apology, or "see you soon." Just, "be waiting."

I chastised myself.

What did I expect? He *owns* me—he doesn't *owe* me anything.

Me: Yes, Sir. I'll be waiting.

I kept my phone in my hand in case he responded, but of course, he didn't.

When we pulled into Jeff's drive, I let out a sigh of relief. It had been the right address.

Toby wished me a pleasant evening as he handed me my bag and waited in the car as I punched in the code Jeff had texted me.

Once the lock turned, I gave him a small wave, then stepped inside.

The familiar scent of the house hit me, and I instantly relaxed. That's when I realized... I was comfortable here.

Good grief. How was that possible?

I carried my bag straight to the guest room that I'd been using and shut the door behind me. After stripping quickly, I folded my clothes and set them on the chair in the corner, then pulled a white t-shirt from my bag and slipped it over my head. I was still following the rules—my holes were available to him.

The shirt barely covered my ass. I didn't care. I just didn't want to sit around completely naked while I waited for him to come home.

I went downstairs to the kitchen and opened the refrigerator. A small smile spread across my face when I noticed the stash of Pellegrino bottles he had on a shelf. I grabbed the bottle of Pinot Grigio he'd opened last weekend. He'd said he'd bought it at the winery in Napa Valley where it was made.

I took my glass into the living room and settled onto the couch with my phone to see if he'd texted again.

He hadn't.

I sipped. Waited. And refilled my glass.

As I was walking back into the living room, I remembered the lingerie I had packed.

I'd brought it last week but hadn't had an opportunity to wear it. Tonight seemed like an appropriate time.

I carried my wineglass back upstairs and set it on the dresser as I changed into the sheer black lace teddy I'd gotten on the sale rack. I thought the subtlety of it made it sexier.

I pushed my boobs up so they were spilling out of the cups, then smoothed my hands down the sides of my hips, while I checked myself out in the mirror.

Not bad, I thought, as I put my hands on my waist and turned side to side to see myself from different angles.

I picked up my now-empty wineglass and headed back downstairs. The Pinot was already making me feel warm, but I thought I'd have a little more as I waited.

As I passed through the living room on the way to the kitchen, I noticed a candle on the bookshelf and decided to use the Aim-n-Flame next to the fireplace to light it.

Then I saw another on the end table.

And another on the mantel.

By the time I stepped back and looked around, the whole room glowed in soft light. It was romantic as fuck; the only thing missing was soft music.

That's when I spotted the Bose speaker on the side table. I picked up my phone and tapped Bluetooth. It connected without a password, which to me, seemed like serendipity.

Without thinking too hard, I opened my music app and scrolled to a playlist labeled *Late Nights*.

A slow, sexy song poured out of the speaker, and I sat down on the couch with my wineglass just as I saw lights in the driveway.

****

Jeff

I came into the house through the garage and hung my keys on the hook next to the door before walking further into the house.

I'd hurried home—*not* because I was anxious to see her. But because my cock hadn't been drained in five days, and it was overdue.

That was all.

I was late and was half expecting to find her asleep on the couch, naked. I'd wake her up with my dick in her mouth.

Instead, I walked into the living room and found candlelight and music.

Soft and slow, the kind of song no one plays by accident. The living room glowed. Every flat surface had a candle on it—mantel, end table, bookshelf. The air smelled like candle wax and whatever perfume she wore that had clung to my sheets all week.

She was sitting on the couch in a black lace teddy and holding a glass of wine like she belonged there.

Something tightened in my chest at the sight of her. I liked coming home to this. For a split second, I didn't move, I just looked at her.

And then the second passed.

She didn't live here. She wasn't my girlfriend, and this wasn't a date night.

This was a transaction. She was being paid to be here.

"I didn't realize I was coming home to a Hallmark movie," I quipped as I moved further inside the room.

She looked around with that damn smile I was becoming addicted to.

"Sorry, I went a little overboard."

My voice was cold when I replied, "I don't recall you asking if this would be okay."

Her smile faltered, but she held her ground.

"I just thought—" she started.

"That's the problem," I cut in. "You're here so I can use your holes, not to think, and definitely not to cover up what belongs to me."

Her mouth opened slightly and her eyes widened. I'd pissed her off.

Good.

She set her glass down with a thud, then went about blowing out the candles without a word. The room went eerily quiet when she killed the music; smoke filled the air.

She whirled around and glared at me, then gestured to the lingerie she had on.

She was a goddamn knockout.

"Is this okay, or should I take it off?"

I shrugged like it didn't matter. "I don't care as long as your holes are available."

The muscle in her jaw clenched as she continued glaring at me. The silence was tangible yet her look spoke volumes.

Stepping past me, she bent over the arm of the couch and spread her legs wide. The sight of her pretty pink pussy peeking from the crotch of the teddy caused every coherent thought in my head to flee.

Fuck. She might not be naked, but she'd obeyed my rule.

Her tone was flat when she looked back over her shoulder and asked, "Would you prefer another hole, Sir?"

That was better. She needed to be reminded what this was. Hell, *I* needed to be reminded of it.

I gruffly replied, "No, that hole will work just fine."

I didn't hesitate, just unzipped. Stepping behind her, I grabbed her hips, kicked her legs wider and pushed into her in one rough thrust.

No foreplay. No words. Just the sound of skin meeting skin. Her steady breathing was the only thing that told me she was still with me.

This wasn't about connection, it was about control.

About reminding her—and myself—what this was.

"You think candles and soft music change anything?" I growled as I slammed into her deep. "You think a bit of lace makes you my girlfriend?"

She didn't answer. Her fingers just gripped the cushion tighter.

"Let me make it real clear, slut. You're a warm hole. That's all."

I drove into her harder after that. Meaner. Pretending that punishing her would erase how many times I'd thought about her this week. Or that I'd liked coming home to her.

When I came, I stayed deep, gripping her hips so hard she'd feel it tomorrow.

She didn't make a sound. Didn't move. Merely stayed there like she thought any shift might set me off again.

Then I heard her whisper, "I'm sorry. I just thought you might like to come home to something nice."

Her head hung down so I couldn't see her face, but her voice cracked at the end.

Fuck.

I pulled out and backed away with my fists tight at my sides.

I didn't say anything; just went to the half bath and grabbed a towel.

She was still bent over when I came back and still refused to look at me.

I knelt and cleaned her up, wiping between her thighs and down the backs of her legs. My hands were gentle, but my jaw was locked the whole time.

When I picked her up, I didn't think. Just acted.

Her cheek was damp where it rested against my chest as I carried her up the stairs, making me feel like a bigger asshole than I already did.

I opened my bedroom door and threw the comforter back, then laid her down and pulled the covers up around her.

She didn't say a word.

Neither did I. But I didn't leave.

I sat on the edge for a second, then stripped off my shirt and slid in beside her.

She didn't look at me, but she didn't pull away either.

I wrapped an arm around her and pulled her against my chest, then kissed the top of her head.

I wanted to apologize. God, I wanted to say something. But I didn't.

She was my whore; I shouldn't give a shit about hurting her feelings.

This was a transaction. Sex for money. Nothing else.

I closed my eyes and let myself believe it.

Chapter Twenty-Two

Vivian

My bladder woke me up, and I rolled out of bed to tiptoe to the bathroom.

Except the door wasn't in its usual spot.

That's when I realized I was in Jeff's room, wearing the black lingerie I'd put on last night while waiting for him, and the events of last night came flooding back.

I didn't even want to use the jerk's bathroom, but my need to go overruled my pride, and I slipped in and quietly closed the door before turning the light on.

I'd become used to his cruelty; hell, I'd even been turned on by it. But last night had been different. He'd been angry because he thought I was acting like we were on a date.

To be fair, I could see how from his point of view, it could have looked like that. Maybe I had overstepped. But he'd handled it like a complete asshole.

His only saving grace was he'd seemed remorseful and had apologized in his own way. I knew better than to think he'd actually verbalize an "I'm sorry."

I guess for a hundred thousand dollars, he didn't have to.

The electronic blinds were open when I went back into the bedroom, and Jeff was sitting up in bed, reading something on his phone.

"Good morning," I said softly from the bathroom doorway. I wasn't sure if I should climb back in bed or go to my room and was hoping for some direction from him.

He looked up and smiled. "Good morning."

Okay, so much for that.

I pointed toward the hall. "I'll just go to my room."

His mouth turned down, like he was disappointed. "You can stay if you want, but I understand if you'd rather be alone this morning."

No, I didn't want to be alone.

I wanted to snuggle up next to him and have him pet my hair and tell me I was pretty. Because I was fucked up in the head.

Textbook daddy issues.

"I don't want to bother you."

"You won't bother me." He threw back the comforter on my side and patted the mattress. "Come lie down."

I didn't have to be told twice and slid into bed, although I was careful to stay on my side. I still had no idea where things stood between us.

He didn't let me. He reached over and pulled me into his arms. Once I was situated against his chest, he murmured, "That's better," and continued reading whatever was on his phone.

Meanwhile, butterflies felt they were going to take flight in my stomach.

****

Jeff

I wasn't reading. I hadn't been able to comprehend a word since she got out of bed, and I opened my phone to try and keep my mind occupied.

She'd come out of the bathroom and looked at me like she wasn't sure if she was welcome back in bed, and that bothered me.

I'd pulled her to my side on instinct. She felt right in my arms, even if I wasn't supposed to admit that. Even if I still hated myself a little for how shitty I'd treated her last night, I wasn't going to miss an opportunity to feel good with her naked in my arms.

I glanced down. She was curled into me, soft and warm, with her hair brushing my collarbone.

I should've said something. Asked if she slept okay. If she was sore. If she hated me.

Instead, I just kept staring at my phone like it held the answer.

She was quiet, but I could feel the tension in her body, as if she was thinking about something. Debating.

She shifted once, and I thought she was going to speak, but she didn't. Then she did it again, but still nothing.

Finally, the third time, she whispered, "Why were you so mad last night?"

I didn't answer right away. Mostly because I wasn't sure how to. Or maybe I did and didn't want to say it out loud.

"I don't know," I said. "I walked in and saw everything, and it felt like... too much."

She didn't move. Just waited.

"It looked like something it wasn't. Something it couldn't be."

She was quiet for a second. Then: "A date."

"Yeah."

She didn't say anything else, but I could feel the question behind her silence.

I ran my hand through my hair. "I've had someone do that before. The whole fantasy. Candles, wine, lingerie, the works. It made it feel like something real."

I paused before continuing, "She left me for someone with a trust fund. The funny thing was, I have one too. I just hadn't told her because I wanted her to want me, not my money."

Her breath caught slightly, but she didn't interrupt.

"I was twenty-one and dumb. I thought I'd found the real thing. Reality knocked me on my ass. That's when I realized that most women are for sale to the highest bidder."

She interjected. "Not all women."

"The ones who like it rough don't come free. And we've already established that's how I like it."

It wasn't like she could argue. She was living proof that was true.

That old bitterness crept in, even now.

"So, yeah," I said. "I don't do 'ambiance'. I don't do pretend. If I'm paying for it, I want to be clear on what I'm paying for. Last night blurred that line too much."

She didn't say anything; just quietly lay there against me.

I should've let the conversation die, but I glanced at the phoenix tattoo on her wrist. The one I'd asked about the first night we met, but she wouldn't elaborate on.

Knowing a little more of her story, I could piece together the significance, but I wanted to hear it from her.

My thumb drifted over the ink. "You told me this was a conversation for another time. How about now?"

****

Vivian

I remember he'd asked at the masquerade party, and I'd brushed him off. I didn't normally share my story with people I knew, let alone strangers.

But he wasn't a stranger anymore. Not really. And now he was asking again, and it felt different this time. Like he wasn't just curious. Like he actually cared.

I looked at the ink on my wrist that I'd traced more times than I could count.

"I got it when I was seventeen. The day I'd saved up enough money to sign the lease on my first apartment."

"How were you able to sign a contract at seventeen? Or get a tattoo?"

I shrugged. "I had a fake ID. And the places I frequented didn't exactly scrutinize it."

He nodded like he understood, although I didn't see how he could. Our lives couldn't be more different if we tried.

Still, his thumb traced over it again, slower this time, and he murmured, "My little phoenix. You are a survivor, that's for sure."

Maybe he understood more than I gave him credit for.

Chapter Twenty-Three

Vivian

I showered, then wandered into the kitchen in one of Jeff's white t-shirts. He was leaning against the counter, barefoot, in a red SDSU t-shirt and grey sweats, scrolling through his phone.

He smiled when he glanced up and noticed me, then asked, "Are you hungry?"

I nodded, not sure if I was supposed to assume the position on the island counter.

He opened the fridge and pulled out eggs and sourdough. "Have you ever made French toast?"

I blinked. "Isn't it just bread and eggs?"

He gave a grunt that sounded suspiciously like a laugh. "God help me." Then he reached into a drawer, pulled out an apron, and tossed it to me. "Come here."

I moved immediately to comply.

He showed me how to whisk eggs with cinnamon and vanilla, while explaining why he lets the bread soak instead of dunking it and tossing it on the pan like I probably would've. His hand brushed mine a few times as I worked, but he didn't correct me or take over. Just let me try it myself.

"You're not a bad student," he said when I flipped a piece without mangling it.

"High praise from the Master," I teased.

His brow lifted. "Careful, little girl. That mouth is going to get you in trouble."

"Isn't that what it's for?"

His nostrils flared, and I knew I was about to get fucked on the counter.

And I wasn't mad about it.

****

Jeff

She curled up on the couch next to me. Her cheeks were still flushed, and her hair was messy from where I'd pulled it. A faint handprint lingered on her ass, but she hadn't complained.

She never did.

There was some rom-com on TV that she'd picked out. I'd let her choose it; I thought it was a small concession after the way I'd used her before letting her eat.

She sat close, tucked under my arm like she belonged there. I probably should've made her sit at my feet, but I liked having her by my side.

And that was the problem.

I told myself I was just letting her recharge before I used her again. That it was about control. Ownership.

But the way she tucked her head against my chest?

That didn't feel like submission. It felt like trust.

And I hated how much I liked it.

She laughed quietly at something on the screen, and I looked down to find her wearing a genuine smile. Like this was normal. Like we were just a couple wasting a lazy Saturday.

I should've shut it down right then and told her to move to the floor. Reminded her what this was.

Instead, I pulled her closer and rested my chin on her head.

I was so fucked.

And not in the good way.

****

Vivian

Sunday morning, I woke up in Jeff's bed again, but this time, he was nowhere to be found, and his side of the bed was cold.

I reached over and hugged his pillow, breathing in his scent. We only had one more weekend left together.

But at least I'd get paid the following Monday and be able to put a dent in my dad's debt.

Maybe I'd auction myself again. I doubted I'd bring in another hundred-thousand-dollar bid, but we'd only owe twenty-seven thousand after this. Anything more than that would be gravy.

I let out a bitter laugh.

Only twenty-seven thousand.

There was so much I could do with that kind of money. Get my car window fixed, maybe move into an apartment that wasn't roach-infested, or even take more than one class a semester.

Cherry said she made six figures selling herself. Could I do that, too?

I wasn't so sure. I obviously fell in love too easily, since I was pretty positive I was head over heels for Jeff and was going to be crushed when this came to an end next Sunday night.

I'd either end up heartbroken a lot or jaded. Probably both.

As shitty an example as my parents had set on what marriage looked like, I still wanted to hold on to the dream.

So, no. Once I got us out from the loan-shark debt, I wouldn't be doing this again.

But damn, I had enjoyed sex with Jeff and wondered if it'd ever be that good again. Even though he'd been kinder when we weren't both naked, he'd still treated me like his property when his cock was out. And I'd been more than happy to comply.

I went into the guest room and hopped in the shower to wash his cum from my thighs. And face. And hair.

Maybe I was pathetic for liking it, and maybe, possibly, probably, being in love with him, but I'd come to know both sides of him. And I liked both.

I came out of the bathroom wrapped in a towel and found him sitting on the guest room bed.

"Towel off."

I didn't hesitate to let it drop to my feet and stand there naked for him to look at.

And he did. He took his time perusing me from head to toe before he commanded, "Get on the bed and spread your legs."

Again, I immediately did as instructed. My mind raced with what could possibly be in store for me.

He gave a sinister chuckle, the one I'd come to crave, then ran his finger down my seam.

"You dirty whore. You're already wet."

Then he did something he'd never done. He brought his fingers to his mouth, and said, "Mmm, your cunt tastes good. I think I'll have some more."

I had to spread my legs wider to accommodate his broad shoulders as he positioned himself between my thighs. He didn't waste any time running his tongue through my folds.

I gasped out loud and bowed my back off the bed.

In response, he pinned my hips in place with one arm and attacked my clit with his tongue while pumping two fingers in and out of me.

I let out a long moan, and despite being held in place, tried to grind against his face.

Smack!

He landed a sharp slap to my clit.

"Don't *even think* about coming until I tell you."

"Yes, Sir," I panted.

Another smack landed on my clit.

"You did think about it."

"I'm sorry, Sir. It just feels so good."

He sucked my little nub between his lips and flicked his tongue while he fingered me. I was in sensory overload heaven.

I reached down to grab his hair and hold his face tight against my pussy, then thought better of it, and ran my fingers through his thick hair instead.

"Please, Sir. Can I come?"

I expected him to tell me no, but instead, he snarled, "Come, whore."

My body responded accordingly, and I went from every muscle in my body being constricted, to shuddering in climax. Then my limbs felt like they were made of gelatin.

He leaned down and kissed me—also a first, although I think it was more so he could make me taste myself.

God, I was going to miss this.

My arm wove around his neck as I kissed him back. Our tongues danced and sparred, and as usual, he won control.

And I happily gave it.

****

Jeff

She was packing her bag in the guest room, while I stayed in the living room and scrolled through my phone, trying to occupy my thoughts.

I had to tell myself to unclench my jaw as I waited for her. I'd fucking come to loathe Sunday nights.

She came downstairs a few minutes later in another long-sleeved dress, this one a cobalt blue that matched her eyes. Her collar was in place, and I'd be willing to bet my last dime that she wasn't wearing any underwear.

I got up to meet her at the door, and skimmed my hand along her ass, just to doublecheck.

"Good girl," I murmured in her ear with a smile.

She looked up and replied, "I do learn, ya know."

"I know you do."

The club car pulled into the drive, and I wanted to go punch the driver for being on time.

Her eyes flicked to the window by the door when she saw the headlights, then back to me. "I guess I'll see you Friday."

I nodded once.

She turned to go, but I caught her wrist and pulled her into me.

Then I fucking kissed her forehead.

What the hell am I doing?

I think she must have wondered the same thing, because she blinked up at me with her eyes wide, like she'd been caught off guard.

"Have a good week," I said, and smacked her ass, 'cuz, ya know, that would negate what I'd just done. (Insert eyeroll here.)

She nodded and walked out the door.

And I stood there in the doorway watching her get in the car, then waved when she pulled away.

The entire time wishing I had enough balls just to ask her to stay.

Chapter Twenty-Four

Vivian

I met Kit for an early dinner on Thursday before my evening shift. She picked a taco place that had cheap margaritas, and even though I never drank before or during work, I didn't mind. The food was decent, and it wasn't far from Club Allure, so I could head there once we were done. Plus, it was the kind of place where no one cared if you wore glittery stripper lashes while sitting at the bar or had a collar tucked beneath your hoodie.

"I still can't believe he put you in his bed," she said, dunking a chip into salsa. "That's like, emotional intimacy, Viv. Are you sure he's not catching feelings?"

I snorted as I picked a chip from the basket in front of us. "He told me I was nothing but a warm hole two nights ago. I think it's safe to say that no, he's not catching feelings."

"Yeah, but *after* that, he tucked you in next to him in bed like a goddamn husband. So, which is it?"

"I don't know," I said as I chewed thoughtfully. "He's hot and cold. One minute, I think he might actually like me. The next, he's reminding me I'm just a whore he paid for."

"He paid *a lot of money* for," my BFF murmured under her breath. "Has he texted you?"

I shook my head. "No. But he only texted that one time last week. I don't expect him to."

"And this weekend will fulfill the contract."

"Yep, come seven a.m. Monday morning, sixty grand is supposed to hit my account."

"I want to go piss on your dad's grave for doing this to you. Think of all the things you could do with that money if you didn't have a loan shark to pay."

I sighed. "I have, trust me. I think if the club will let me, I might do another auction to try to get the rest so I'm out from under this shit."

Kit narrowed her eyes. "Do you think Jeff would bid on you again?"

I shrugged, trying to pretend the thought didn't appeal to me as much as it did.

"I'm not sure. He might be ready for this to be over."

"Do you have to give him the collar back?"

I tilted my head. "I don't know. He didn't say."

"But you're going to quit wearing it after Sunday, right?"

The thought made me sad, but I knew it'd be weird if I didn't.

"I mean, yeah. I'll no longer "belong" to him."

I made air quotes around "belong."

She finished the last of her margarita and signaled to the bartender for another.

"I hope your heart gets that memo."

Yeah, me too.

****

Jeff

I made a decision, then plucked my car key from the hook and opened the garage door, intending to drive to her place before I chickened out.

I was going to ask Vivian to keep seeing me. Not because we had a contract and she was getting paid, but because she wanted to spend time with me as my... girlfriend?

I winced as the word entered my head, but had to concede—yeah, that's what I wanted. Sometime between Sunday night when I went to bed alone and tonight when I walked into an empty house, I realized I'd fallen for Vivian... *Holy shit, I didn't even know her last name.*

Then another thought hit me. *What if she'd only been pretending to like me because she was getting paid?*

I gave myself an internal shake. No, I'd seen the way she'd looked at me. The way she'd smiled when she'd been snuggled up against me. She felt the same.

I pulled out of my garage and pulled up the app linked to her collar. The dot blinked steady on the map, and I tapped the screen to expand the location, then frowned.

Club Allure?

What the fuck was she doing at a strip club?

I took a deep breath even as my fingers clenched around the steering wheel as I drove.

I needed to give her the benefit of the doubt.

Maybe she was bartending. Or helping a friend. Or picking someone up. I shouldn't jump to conclusions. But her location never moved the whole drive over.

I pulled into the lot, turned the car off and sat looking at the red neon sign and the line of men waiting while the bouncer checked IDs. Had I been sharing my little whore with other men this whole time?

I guess I was about to find out.

I got out of the car, clicked the lock, and headed toward the entrance.

The bouncer waved me through with a nod, and I stepped inside. It took a second for my eyes to adjust to the lights while the bass of the music for the girl grinding on a pole onstage pumped through the speakers.

I looked at the bar first, trying to keep with the whole "giving her the benefit of the doubt" theme. She wasn't there.

But it didn't take long to find her.

She was in a corner booth, perched in some asshole's lap with her arms looped around his neck and her tits practically in his face. She wasn't smiling, not really, but she wasn't faking it either.

She was working.

Just not for me.

Her head turned, and our eyes locked.

Time stopped.

Her body stilled, but she didn't get off the guy. She didn't move at all. She just stared at me like I'd caught her cheating—even though she hadn't made me any promises.

Even though I hadn't asked her to.

I held her gaze as another dancer walked by, this one brunette and leggy, wearing glitter heels, red pasties and a matching red thong that barely covered anything.

"Hey, baby," she purred, brushing her hand across my chest.

I didn't look at her, just kept my eyes locked on Vivian and said, loud enough for her to hear, "You free for a private room?"

Vivian flinched.

The brunette grinned. "Of course. The Champagne Room is three hundred for fifteen minutes."

I nodded, still staring at the girl I was trying to emotionally gut, like she'd just gutted me. I finally glanced at the girl in front of me and smiled. "You're so fucking hot, I'll only need ten. Lead the way, beautiful."

Then I let the stranger lead me away by the hand, knowing full well Vivian was watching as I went behind a red velvet curtain.

****

Vivian

I felt like I was going to vomit as Jeff held Sapphire's hand and walked toward the Champagne Room. He looked back and gave me an evil grin just before he stepped inside without a moment's hesitation.

My bottom lip quivered, but I tightly pressed that bitch against my top one. I refused to let the bastard see me cry.

With a too-bright smile, I apologized and told the guy whose dick was poking me through my G-string that I'd give him another half a song.

I tried my best, but the dude did not get his twenty bucks worth. My rhythm was off, and all I could think about was Jeff pushing Sapphire's head down on his cock and telling her to swallow every drop.

That motherfucker.

I slid off the dude I was grinding on and muttered something about needing a break, then made my way to the bar.

The older bartender gave me a smile. "You doing all right, Crystal? Do I need to get one of the bouncers?"

Oooh, that'd be fun. Watching Jeff get tossed out on his ass by the meatheads working security in the yellow shirts wearing earpieces.

Still, I'd have a hard time explaining how Jeff had hassled me when he hadn't even talked to me.

"Hey, Frank. No, nothing like that. I just need some water."

The music kept going, girls paraded onto the stage and performed while men ogled them. In other words, the world kept turning. Meanwhile, I felt like it'd stopped.

I'd just finished my water when I saw Jeff come out from behind the curtain, zipping up his pants, and looking around. I knew exactly what—or rather, who—he was looking for.

Me.

His eyes finally found mine, and he patted Sapphire's ass when she walked past him, then glanced back to make sure I was still watching. He smirked when he saw I had been.

I didn't break eye contact as I reached up to my throat, unclasped the collar, slid it off my neck, and held it up for him to see it dangling from my fingertips.

I glared at him as if to say, *You wanted a performance? Here's your fucking encore, prick.*

I closed my hand around it, then I turned on the ball of my foot and walked backstage with my head held high.

At least until I reached the dressing room.

That's where I burst into tears.

I didn't bother to change, just threw a sweatshirt on over my head with pasties still on my tits and wriggled into my jeans over my G-string. I grabbed my bag and pulled on my coat before heading out the back door to the employee parking lot.

I watched in the dark from the driver's seat of my Malibu, with tears still streaming down my face, as he slid behind the wheel of his Porsche and drove off like he didn't have a care in the world.

Only then did I start my car and head toward Kit's apartment.

Chapter Twenty-Five

Vivian

Kit took one look at my face when she answered the door and just stepped aside to let me pass, then wrapped her arms around me and didn't let go.

"That fucker's going to get the most watered-down drinks from now on," she promised. "From everyone. I'll spread the word."

I laughed through my tears. It wasn't really much of a consolation since it meant he'd be back at the club.

"You can hide out here as long as you need to, babe. I've got your back."

~ ~ ~ ~

When my phone buzzed with a text on Friday at precisely five p.m., I knew exactly who it was.

Jeff: The driver is waiting. Don't make me tell him to leave.

Was he fucking for real?

Did he actually think I'd go to his house after what he did to me at *my* club? I hadn't been able to figure out how he knew I'd be there. Hell, maybe he hadn't known, and he'd gone there for entertainment. Seeing me had just been a coincidence.

Yet somehow, I was the bad guy.

Fuck him.

Me: You probably should since I'm not home.

I flipped my phone face down on the coffee table and kept folding Kit's laundry. I wasn't going. And I wasn't explaining myself either.

Two minutes later, my phone buzzed again.

Jeff: If you don't show up tonight, the contract is null and void.

Me: Then I guess it's null and void.

My stomach twisted at the thought of losing out on that money, but there was no way I could bring myself to go tonight.

Let him be pissed. Let him report me to the club if he wanted. I didn't care.

Except I did.

I stacked the last towel on the pile and told myself I wasn't going to cry again. My eyes were still puffy from my sob session last night and again this morning, even after putting frozen spoons on them.

My phone buzzed again, only this time the message was from Kit.

Kit: How are you holding up?

Me: He just told me if I don't show up, the contract is null and void. Which means I get nothing.

Kit: You sure you want to walk from sixty grand? It's just one more weekend.

Me: I can't do it, Kit. He humiliated me in front of everyone I work with.

Kit: Yeah, but did they know what was happening?

Me: I'm sure Sapphire must have, and she probably told everyone else by the end of the night.

Kit: I'm all for some light vandalism when I get home. A rock through a window. Maybe some spray paint on his garage...

God, I loved her.

Me: I'll think about it, but for now, I'm going to curl up in a ball and cry some more.

Kit: He's not worth your tears, babe. Order a pint of ice cream and a bottle of wine from Instacart and put on a horror flick. DO NOT WATCH A ROMCOM! Tomorrow we're getting mani/pedis.

Me: I love you so much. Thank you for letting me crash here for another night.

Kit: You did my laundry. You're welcome any time!

I wasn't going to overstay my welcome, but I did want to spend a little extra time with her. I'd been thinking about what Mom, Hope, and I were going to do come Tuesday when I didn't have the big payment we'd promised Lorenzo. As much as it sucked, the only feasible option was to skip town for a while.

Maybe a fresh start would do us all good.

~~~~

"Are you okay?" Hope asked from the couch, curled up with her knees under her chin and a mug of cocoa in her hands.

I nodded, even though I wasn't. I doubted I ever would be again.

Mom walked into the living room and did a doubletake when she looked at me.

"Viv, what's wrong?"

I'd come over Sunday evening after spending all weekend trying to figure out how I was going to tell my family I hadn't been able to come up with the money for Lorenzo after all.

I'd never explained how I was getting a big influx of cash, and they were both street-savvy enough to know not to ask.

"I think we might need to start thinking about leaving town," I said, keeping my voice low.

Hope's face fell. "You couldn't get the money?"

"No," I replied with a sad smile. "The deal fell through."

Mom didn't say anything, but the look she gave me was the same one she used to give Dad when he'd blow half his paycheck at the casino. Tired, wary.

I continued on, trying to sound pragmatic. "You can crash at my place tomorrow. If I work a double, I should be able to make enough for traveling money."

Maybe I'd even work the Champagne Room.

I had no doubt that wherever we landed, I could get another job dancing. The problem was, we needed gas money to make it there first.

I bit back a sob when I told them, "I'm sorry."
I was sorry about so many fucking things.

Chapter Twenty-Six

Vivian

The chime of a bank alert woke me at exactly seven a.m., and I lay with my eyes closed tight, not wanting to look. But then I realized there was no way I was overdrawn, I hadn't spent any money.

My account better not have gotten hacked again. I groaned at the thought.

I knew I wouldn't be able to fall back asleep until I faced this head-on, so, still groggy, I fumbled for my phone on the nightstand. Then blinked at the screen.

I rubbed the sleep from my eyes and blinked again.

The message hadn't changed.

Deposit: $60,000
Description: ZRE Enterprises

I sat up straight, my heart pounding.

I knew Kit's paychecks came from ZRE Enterprises. They owned Velvet Underground.

That had to be a mistake. The contract was null and void. Jeff had said so himself. I wasn't entitled to anything.

I stared at the number as I tried to make sense of how this could have happened. The only thing I could come up with was someone must not have entered that Jeff had canceled our agreement before they paid me.

One thing was certain; I needed to get my ass to the bank and withdraw that money before ZRE Enterprises had a chance to reverse the deposit.

I was going to be waiting at the bank's door when they unlocked it at nine a.m.

I'd rather owe a sex club sixty thousand than a guy named Lorenzo who'd threatened my mom's fingers and the family dog. I think the worst Velvet Underground would do was make me work the debt off. Either that or send me to collections.

Big whoop.

~~~~

I double-checked the address as I pulled into the lot. The building looked more like a mechanic's shop than a place where backroom deals went down. Although, I guess I wasn't sure what that should look like.

I parked, shut off the engine, and double-checked the envelope was still in my purse, even though I'd driven there straight from the bank, so I didn't know where it would have gone.

My heart rate had kicked up with each thousand the teller had counted out, but it wasn't exactly like I could ask for a cashier's check. Who would I have had them make it out to? Lorenzo's Loan Shark Services?

I'd stuffed the envelope in my purse, then looked around as though the police might appear to arrest me as soon as I walked away from the bank window.

That wasn't my money, and I knew it.

I got out of the Malibu and muttered, "Too late now."

Inside, the waiting room was empty except for a peeling green vinyl couch and a guy behind a glass window who looked annoyed he had to pause the game on his phone to talk to me.

"I need to speak to Lorenzo," I said.

He gave me a once-over, then buzzed a door open without saying a word.

Lorenzo was exactly as my sister had described him, minus the two goons. His small office had no windows, and the air smelled like a mixture of cigarettes and cologne.

He didn't acknowledge me when I entered, just kept flipping through scraps of paper in a manila folder until I cleared my throat.

I tried to sound confident when I said, "I'm here to make a payment on Ray Dempsey's loan," but my shaking knees might have given me away.

He didn't even look up. "Loan's been paid in full."

I blinked. "Excuse me?"

Finally, he looked at me. Of course, he talked to my chest when he replied, "Guy came in yesterday and covered the entire amount."

My mouth went dry. "Did he leave a name?"

His gaze finally climbed to my face, slow and smug, and made my skin want to crawl. "Nope. Porsche. Nice watch. Sound like your sugar daddy?"

I stared at him while my heartbeat was in my ears. Now was not the time to try and unpack why Jeff would have done something like this.

"Are we done, then?" I asked as I took a step back before he even answered.

"We're done," he said, then opened the folder back up. "You're free and clear."

Maybe as far as this debt went. But I had a feeling the other shoe was going to drop soon enough.

Chapter Twenty-Seven

Vivian

I still wasn't sure if Velvet Underground was going to demand their money back, so I showed up to work for my usual Monday evening shift.

I was fixing my lashes in the mirror backstage when Sapphire sauntered up beside me, chewing on a piece of gum and watching me through the reflection.

"So," she said, too casually, "you and your boyfriend make up yet?"

I paused, my lip gloss wand halfway to my mouth. "He's not my boyfriend."

She gave a snort. "Sure looked like you gave a damn when he left with me the other night."

I turned to face her fully, ready to tell her to mind her own business, but her expression surprised me. It wasn't smug—it was almost... apologetic?

"For what it's worth," she said, "he didn't touch me."

I felt my brows furrow. "What?"

"In the Champagne Room. He didn't want a dance. Didn't want anything." She tucked a piece of hair behind her ear. "Just asked about you."

Wait, what?

"He seemed pissed," she added. "But not at me."

I didn't know what to say to that.

Sapphire shrugged. "Figured you'd want to know."

Then she walked off, leaving me staring at my reflection. I didn't know what to think, and there was only one way to find out for sure.

****

Jeff

The doorbell rang just after eight.

I wasn't expecting anyone, although I dared to hope it'd be her when I opened the door.

And as if I'd conjured her up, there she was, standing on my doorstep in a hoodie, jeans, and tennis shoes, without a stitch of makeup on.

She didn't say anything at first. Just stared at me with her big, blue eyes. I wasn't sure if she was about to punch me or kiss me. Instead, she slowly pulled something from her pocket. It was a white envelope. One that bore a bank name and contained something thick. I was pretty certain I knew what that was.

She held it out and finally, she spoke, her tone demanding when she asked, "Why did the club pay me? This isn't mine, it's yours."

Ignoring the envelope, I leaned one shoulder against the frame, shook my head, and keeping my voice calm, said, "It's yours. You earned it."

Her expression showed her disagreement, eyes revealing the internal battle I was sure she was having with herself. The victor was determined as she shoved the envelope back into her pocket and though, she crossed her arms, her tone softened. "And Lorenzo? That debt my dad owed? Why did you pay him?"

I didn't answer right away. Just looked at her. Her arms dropped, fingers fidgeting nervously in the front pocket of her hoodie as she stared back at me.

"You know why I did it."

Her voice dropped to barely a whisper. "I need to hear you say it."

I swallowed hard, then gave her the truth. "Because I love you. Because I wanted you to come back, but only if you were free. Only if you wanted to."

For a second, I thought she might bolt. Her eyes glistened, and she looked down. Then she pulled something out of the same pocket where she'd just stashed the envelope—her collar.

"Am I still your whore?" she asked.

I stepped forward and gently took the jewelry from her and put it around her neck.

"Only if you want to be," I murmured in her ear as I secured the clasp.

Her hand went to her neck, like she was double-checking it was on. "I do. But I want to be more than that."

I cupped her face in my hands as I stared into her eyes.

"You are, baby. You're not just mine on the weekends anymore. You're mine. Period."

She nodded her head as the first tear spilled down her cheek. "I want that, too."

I gave her a wicked grin, grabbed a fistful of her hair, pulled her inside, and replied, "Good. Now get on your knees."

"Yes, Sir," she whispered as she dropped to the floor. "Yours."

Epilogue

Three months later
Jeff

We didn't come here for the sex.

Not anymore.

Vivian sat perched in my lap in a booth at Velvet Underground, a little smirk on her lips while we watched Grayson swoop in on a woman I'd never seen before. Two minutes later, he was escorting her toward the private suites.

She leaned in. "Damn, he's got game."

I kissed her temple. "He didn't with you."

She sipped her bourbon and rolled her eyes. "Neither did you that night."

My hand slid between her legs. "But I own you now. Do I need to remind you of that by putting you back on the table and showing everyone again who you belong to?"

Her pupils dilated, but she shook her head.

"No, once was enough."

We only came back because my membership was already paid through the end of the year, and Vivian missed Kit.

That was the excuse, anyway.

The truth? We liked watching. Together. And, on occasion, being watched.

There was power in knowing no one here could touch her. That even when they watched, they only got the show.

The real thing belonged to me, forever—if she said yes when I asked her on her birthday in June.

Highest Bidder

****

The next morning
Vivian

Jeff said I wasn't allowed to touch his espresso machine. So obviously, I touched it.

I was still half-asleep, standing in his—our—kitchen, wearing nothing but his wrinkled shirt from the night before and a little dried cum he'd left on my thighs. My ass was sore. My throat ached in the most satisfied way, and my hair smelled like his cologne.

In other words, I felt perfect.

I'd almost figured out the grind setting when Bear—our black, fuzzy rescue mutt who fit his name—nudged my hand with his nose.

"Good morning, buddy," I cooed as I bent to scratch behind his ears. He licked my hand, then went out the doggy door Jeff had installed the day after we brought him home from the pound.

I returned to fiddling with the machine just as Jeff sauntered in, shirtless and already frowning.

"You know better."

"I was gentle."

He stepped behind me, crowding my space. His hand wrapped around mine, guiding the portafilter into place. "You're not gentle with *anything*."

"You like that about me."

"I love that about you."

I froze.

We didn't say it often. Not out loud. But he'd said it like breathing this time—easy and automatic.

He kissed the back of my neck. "I mean it."

I closed my eyes and leaned my back against his front. "I love you too."

I still had a hard time believing I could say that out loud.

He reached up and squeezed my boob while murmuring in my ear, "You're still not allowed to touch the machine."

I smiled. "Too late."

He growled. *Growled.* Then yanked the mug from my hand and set it on the counter.

"I'm going to have to punish you."

"Oh no! Not a punishment!" I mocked. "Whatever shall I do?"

He pushed the shirt up my back and bent me over the counter without another word.

This was my life now. No more stripping. No more scraping to get by. I was in school full-time, and for the first time I could ever remember, I was excited about my future.

Men might still see me at Velvet Underground—watch me sip bourbon in Jeff's lap, half-dressed with his hand between my legs—but only one of them ever got to touch.

And right now, he was fucking me over the kitchen counter before his first cup of coffee.

****

Jeff originally appears as a good guy with a hint of a darker side in *Sloane*. Get it here!

https://tesssummersauthor.com/sloane

Thank You

Thank you for reading *Highest Bidder*!

I know this isn't my usual good guy for a hero story, but I wanted to try something new.

As I worked on this, I told Maggie, my editor, that I wasn't sure if I needed therapy or church, or both.

But you know what? It was fun to write, and I hope it was fun for you to read! Unless this absolutely flops, I'm going to continue the series. Grayson DeLuca's story will be next.

Will you consider leaving me a review wherever you purchased this book? And, if it's not too much trouble, Goodreads and/or BookBub? (And even if you didn't like the story, I'd be grateful if you left your [gentle] thoughts.)

Don't forget to sign up for my newsletter to get tons of bonus content for *free*, plus be the first to know about cover reveals, contests, excerpts, and more!

https://www.subscribepage.com/TessSummersNewsletter

xoxo,

Tess

ACKNOWLEDGMENTS

Maggie Ryan: You're just the best. I can't say enough awesome things about you. Thank you for making this book better (even though I know you prefer my good guy books!)

Mr. Summers: Thank you for putting up with me and my inability to do anything else when I've got a deadline looming (that I know I totally did to myself). You are the glue that keeps everything together, and I'd be lost without you. (Plus, who would feed me?)

Kae Popp: I fucking love you. Thank you for making my life easier.

My extended family: I really hope you don't read this book.

Lastly, to my readers: You're the reason I get to be on this crazy journey. Thank you for supporting me through it. I am humbled with every page of mine that you read.

BREAKFAST IS SERVED

She doesn't do sleepovers, let alone relationships. He's going to try and change that.

Lauren's business is her baby—she doesn't have time for relationships. So after a fundraiser when she goes home with her best friend's boss and she's still there in the morning, that's a problem. She doesn't do breakfast with her one-night stands—ever.

Not returning his calls seems like the safest bet. Better not to start something she can't finish.

Except Tristan didn't build one of the most successful law firms in the state by not going after what he wants. And what he wants is Lauren in his bed every night and her in his arms every morning.

More from Tess Summers:

SAN DIEGO SOCIAL SCENE

Operation Sex Kitten: (Ava and Travis)
https://tesssummersauthor.com/operation-sex-kitten
The General's Desire: (Brenna and Ron)
https://tesssummersauthor.com/the-generals-desire
Playing Dirty: (Cassie and Luke)
https://tesssummersauthor.com/playing-dirty
Cinderella and the Marine: (Cooper and Katie)
https://tesssummersauthor.com/cinderella-and-the-marine-1
The Playboy and the SWAT Princess (Craig and Maddie)
https://www.amazon.com/dp/B0CWRQ9PZC
The Heiress and the Mechanic: **(Harper and Ben)**
https://tesssummersauthor.com/heiress-%26-the-mechanic
Burning Her Resolve: (Grace and Ryan)
https://tesssummersauthor.com/burning-her-resolve-1
This Is It: (Paige and Grant)
https://tesssummersauthor.com/this-is-it
Sloane: (Ashley and Sloane)
https://tesssummersauthor.com/sloane

AGENTS OF ENSENADA

Ignition: (Kennedy and Dante prequel)
   https://tesssummersauthor.com/ignition-1
Inferno: (Kennedy and Dante)
   https://tesssummersauthor.com/inferno
Combustion: (Reagan and Mason)
   https://tesssummersauthor.com/combustion-1
Reignited: (Taren and Jacob)
   https://tesssummersauthor.com/reignited
Flashpoint: (Sophia and Ramon)
   https://tesssummersauthor.com/flashpoint

Boston's Elite Series

Wicked Hot Silver Fox
https://tesssummersauthor.com/wicked-hot-silver-fox-1

Wicked Hot Doctor
https://tesssummersauthor.com/wicked-hot-doctor-1

Wicked Hot Medicine
https://tesssummersauthor.com/wicked-hot-medicine

Wicked Hot Baby Daddy
https://tesssummersauthor.com/wicked-hot-baby-daddy

Wicked Bad Decisions
https://tesssummersauthor.com/wicked-bad-decisions-1

Wicked Little Secret
https://tesssummersauthor.com/wicked-little-secret-1

Wicked Grumpy Heart Doc
https://tesssummersauthor.com/wicked-grumpy-heart-doc

Wicked Little Thief
https://tesssummersauthor.com/wicked-little-thief

WOUNDED HEROES

Callahan (Adam and Lainey)
    https://www.amazon.com/dp/B0DB3T9RG1
Sergeant O' (Brian and Jade)
    https://www.amazon.com/dp/B0FCD1MCQG

THE MISTER SERIES

Mr. Infuriating (Gabe and Gretchen)
    https://www.amazon.com/dp/B0F44DB821
Mr. Inappropriate (Bean and...?)
    https://www.amazon.com/dp/B0FFGMSYD1

About the Author

Tess Summers is a former businesswoman and teacher who always loved writing but never seemed to have time to sit down and write a short story, let alone a novel. Now battling MS, her life changed dramatically, and she has finally slowed down enough to start writing all the stories she's been wanting to tell, including the fun and sexy ones!

Married thirty years with three grown children, Tess is a former dog foster mom who ended up failing and adopting them instead (8 times!) She and her husband split their time between the desert of Arizona and the lakes of Michigan, so she's always in a climate that's not too hot and not too cold, but just right!

Contact Me!

Sign up for my newsletter: BookHip.com/SNGBXD
Email: TessSummersAuthor@yahoo.com
Visit my website: www.TessSummersAuthor.com
Facebook: http://facebook.com/TessSummersAuthor
My FB Group: Tess Summers Sizzling Playhouse
TikTok: https://www.tiktok.com/@tesssummersauthor
Instagram: https://www.instagram.com/tesssummers/
Amazon: https://amzn.to/2MHHhdK
BookBub https://www.bookbub.com/profile/tess-summers
Goodreads - https://www.goodreads.com/TessSummers

Made in the USA
Las Vegas, NV
08 July 2025

24626543R00105